LIBRARI
WITHDRAWN FROM STOCK

KU-177-983

Enough *is* Enough *Already*

Carline Francois

TATE PUBLISHING
AND ENTERPRISES, LLC

Enough is Enough Already
Copyright © 2014 by Carline Francois. All rights reserved.

No part of this publication may be reproduced, stored in a retrieval system or transmitted in any way by any means, electronic, mechanical, photocopy, recording or otherwise without the prior permission of the author except as provided by USA copyright law.

The opinions expressed by the author are not necessarily those of Tate Publishing, LLC.

Published by Tate Publishing & Enterprises, LLC
127 E. Trade Center Terrace | Mustang, Oklahoma 73064 USA
1.888.361.9473 | www.tatepublishing.com

Tate Publishing is committed to excellence in the publishing industry. The company reflects the philosophy established by the founders, based on Psalm 68:11,
"The Lord gave the word and great was the company of those who published it."

Book design copyright © 2014 by Tate Publishing, LLC. All rights reserved.
Cover design by Errol Villamante
Interior design by Jake Muelle

Published in the United States of America

ISBN: 978-1-62746-856-5
1. Fiction / Christian
2. Fiction / Coming of Age
14.01.28

Dedication

This book is dedicated to the Lord, my family, those that have had to deal with a loss, life-changing experiences, or finding purpose through faith in the Lord.

Table of Contents

Prologue

I couldn't eat now, but she reminded me that I was eating for two, and I needed to be strong to go see Nick and Dachon. I knew she was right. I ate as much as possible. I told them that Harrington and Maxx were on their way. Mom and Marja were prepping me to go see Nick and Dachon.

They took me to see them. They were both in the same way as I had seen them. Nick's head was wrapped in bandages. Dachon's right leg and left arm were in a cast. Dachon's head was still wrapped in bandages. I walked over to Nick and squeezed his hand. I kissed him on his forehead. I just kept thinking of how much we loved each other. Tears were welling up in my eyes. I still couldn't believe that this was happening. I looked over at Dachon, got up from Nick's bed, and walked over to him. I kissed him on the forehead and held his little hands in mine. I remember rocking him to sleep while telling him little bedtime stories. He would fall asleep in my arms, and now he lay there helpless, and there was nothing I can do but pray that the Lord brings them back to me. I tried to think positively and with optimism. This wasn't easy. I stayed with them through lunch. They still hadn't awakened yet. When the doctor came to see them, I asked the doctor if this was normal for them to not awaken for this long since their surgery. He said yes. He said recovery can take months, and sometimes a patient can lapse into a coma. He said that they are not in a coma but in a sleeping state.

Afternoon came and Maxx had made it to the hospital. Harrington and Nick's parents were on their way. Mom and Marja filled Maxx in on what was happening, which is not much. Maxx came into their room. We greeted each other and hugged. Then he moved over to Nick and kissed him on the forehead. He held Nick's hand. For a brief moment, I thought Nick's hand moved a bit. Maxx then saw his little nephew Dachon on the other bed. He replaced Nick's hand and walked over to his nephew and kissed him on the forehead. He held Dachon's little hand in his. It was a moment of nostalgia. Indescribable. Because our hearts lay on the two beds and, at this moment, time is not ours. We are not in control. Their life hangs at the hands of fate and with faith standing on the background of hope.

I couldn't take it anymore. The hospital had a chapel. I went there to sit with the Lord. What else can I do? I knelt and stared at Risen Lord image over the altar. I prayed to my Risen Lord and asked him if my Nick and Dachon that He gave me as a gift can rise too. I prayed with an aching heart that His will would be done, whichever way it went; I gave thanks to my Risen Lord that I was able to have happy memories with them. I prayed that whichever way it goes that the babe in my womb would be safe, and I thanked the Lord for this little gift of life as well. I gave my Risen Lord my sorrows, my pain and my aching heart. I told Him that in the silence of my faith, I am sad that this happened, and I know somehow all things would work for the greater good. I thanked the Lord for this sense of strength I still feel within. The pains in my lower abdomen were not as bad as before. The pain had subsided. I just sat there in silence. Helpless, but not really. I looked up at the image of my Lord, and with raw heartfelt pleas, I prayed, "Lord, I don't want them to go to heaven yet. I want us to spend more time together. Dachon is only four. Nick loves his community projects. We have our family dream to fulfill. I know heaven is a better place. I just want some more time with them. We love them. In all this, I respect Your will." I knelt before the Lord and said the Lord's Prayer and the Hail Mary and genuflected. I left the chapel and returned to their room.

By this time, Nick's parents and Harrington were in Nick and Dachon's room. I hugged them all and told them I was spending some quiet time at the chapel. Nick's father, Brandon, was sitting with Nick; and Nick's mom, Vera, was sitting with Dachon. They were silent. I left Brandon and Vera alone with Nick and Dachon and went to the lobby to be with the others. On the way to the lobby, I felt a sharp excruciating pain in my lower abdomen. I nearly fell on the floor. Thank goodness a nurse was walking by and held me up. There was a wheelchair that was stationed on the side of the wall of the hallway. She wheeled it over to me and helped me to sit on it. She asked me if I had a room in the hospital. I told her yes and that my family was in the lobby. She wheeled me to the lobby. Harrington came forward, and the nurse told him that I needed to rest because I nearly collapsed in the hallway. Mom, Marja, Maxx, and Harrington took me to my room. They said that I needed to rest, and they would check on Nick and Dachon for me. What could I say? I needed to rest because if I didn't the little baby in my womb would be in danger. I could go to see Nick and Dachon a little later. I rested for about two hours and woke up feeling better. Nick's parents were in my room. "Hi, Brandon and Vera. How are you? Were there any responses from Nick and Dachon? I asked."

Brandon said, "They both have not awakened yet. I did feel Nick squeezing my thumb a little, but Dachon has been the same." Vera was solemn. She smiled at me a little. I could see the worry on her face. I sat up from the bed and reached over to touch her hand. "We just have to stay strong and hope for the best." She nodded yes. Brandon asked what happened *(although they knew from Maxx telling them, I guess they wanted to hear it from me)*. I motioned them to sit down and proceeded to explain to them what happened.

I started from what the police officers informed me about the robbery that led to the car chase to the multiple car accident that resulted. I further explained the aftermath where three people were air lifted to the nearest hospital for emergency surgeries. Nick and Dachon being two of the three. They both sat there in dismay. I told them that I never had the chance to tell Nick that I was pregnant with our child (tears welling up in my eyes). Brandon and Vera got up and came over to me. We hugged with a sense of reassurance and warmth. Then I said, "Let us go see Nick and Dachon." The pain had subsided, and I was able to sit in the wheelchair without help. They wheeled me to Nick and Dachon's room.

While we were there, the nurse came and announced that visiting hours would be over in thirty minutes. I told everyone that they were staying at our house. Mom and Marja were in charge of making sure everyone was settled there for their stay. They both new our house very well, so I knew everyone would be okay. Everyone started to say their good-byes to Nick and Dachon. I myself was wheeled back into my room with instructions that Dr. Chung and Dr. Waverly would be there to check up on me. The nurse in charge of Nick and Dachon said that Dr. Friedman would be in tomorrow morning to check on Nick, and Dr. Waverly would also check on Dachon in the morning as well. I said okay. I just felt like I was at a standstill with nothing to do. You know at this point there really was nothing to do, but be patient and continue visiting them. Everything was in the Lord's hands now. The Lord was giving me strength and peace from within. I gave thanks to Lord and prayed that both Nick and Dachon would pull through with God's grace. With these thoughts in mind, I fell asleep.

Next morning, I woke up early around 5:00 a.m. The hospital room was quiet. I decided to get ready and go visit Nick and Dachon. I missed spending alone time with them. I haven't heard from anyone yet. The pains had subsided while I was freshening up and getting ready. Feeling stronger, I didn't use the wheelchair and walked down to the opposite side of the twelfth floor to the ICU area. The hallway was very quiet. The nurses' station was also quiet. The energy was quiet and serene. At this point, it didn't feel like this was a hospital, which seemed odd for me to think that. As I turned the corner, the scenery changed before me, I saw nurses and doctors coming in and out of Nick and Dachon's hospital room. Here, there was a lot of energy in the area at such an early morning. Approaching their room, I stopped one of the nurses. She recognized me and said, "Oh, Mrs. Oberon, we were just about to come and see you. Mr. Oberon and your son, Dachon, are in distress. We are trying to stabilize them. The doctors are inside doing the best they can to stabilize them."

Where It All Began

Let me see. Where it all began. I don't know. I was at a turning point in my life where I felt my life was not on purpose, as if something was missing. I didn't know what it was. I would often speak to my friend about it until one day she began to ask me about my faith. She would often talk about the Lord, but I didn't really pay to close attention. I mean, I went to church on Sundays, observed Lent (giving up something), Jesus dying on the cross to save us, Easter (Jesus's Resurrection and Him being my Savior), and Christmas (God's plan coming into being with Mary accepting her call to birth Our Savior).

I knew all these, yet I felt that something was missing. My relationship with God was distant somehow. So when my friend started asking me if I had a personal relationship with the Lord, the question was a little unsettling. I don't know. Funny, she asked because the next Sunday I attended Mass, the pastor was talking about having a personal relationship with God through Jesus. Being that it was a week after we celebrated Easter and we were going through the sacred scriptures, it seemed an appropriate message. One of my favorite scriptures was being read. It is the one about the two disciples speaking to this stranger on the road to Emmaus. This time it seemed that the pastor was preaching it differently or maybe I was hearing it differently. He was speaking about a personal encounter and how we can begin to have that personal encounter with the Lord. He was saying how easy it was and it only takes a decision. He went on to say that reconciliation would be the first step. That day seemed to put my thoughts in a new forward-thinking path of discovering this thing called faith. This personal encounter with Christ that the pastor was talking about was interesting. I wanted to know what that was like. I never thought of it before and knew somehow it would help me find that something that was missing. The next time I had a chance, I went to confession to ask the Lord for pardon for my past sins and received absolution from the priest. I did my penance. I did this to renew my faith in the Lord, to let Him know that I wanted a personal relationship with Him. To ask Him to help me live more on purpose. I think He heard my prayer, because things were changing a bit. I began feeling renewed and full of life. It was as if I had a new lease on life or something. It was not just a new lease on life, but it was an inspirational call to a closer relationship with Christ and to know my purpose in Him. I began by attending daily mass-three times per week (I remember reading sacred scripture that the early Christians broke bread daily), reading sacred scripture, and reading the lives of the saints. Doing these increased my faith in Christ and gave me a deeper understanding of Christ's ministry. The Lord's journey through His Passion and Resurrection gave me a deeper understanding as to why and where I fit in. My external life was changing as well. This is something new that I realized too, as one journeys in the faith. (As you grow in faith, your life tends to change with it).

I was going to night school studying to be a Technologist. The classes were really hard and I was struggling and afraid that I would fail. After my spiritual renewal, my classes seemed easier. I was passing my tests and passed my final exam. Graduation came and the ceremony was surreal. It was an amazing moment. It made me happy that one of my dreams was coming true. The following week, I received an invitation from the school to attend their job fair. I made the decision to go, because it was time to start looking for work in this new field.

The day came. I registered at the table and was given a brochure that listed all the companies that would be in attendance at the job fair. While browsing through the brochure, I noticed that the local hospital had an opening for a Technologist. When the time was ready to meet with the companies, I made my way to the table where the local hospital was set up. The recruiter introduced himself and proceeded to tell me about the positions that they were recruiting for. I waited until he was finished and informed him that I was interested in applying for the Technologist position. He proceeded to tell me about the position and the company benefits. I gave him my resume and explained to him that I just graduated as a Technologist. To my surprise we ended up meeting for a mini-interview. The interview went well and a second interview was scheduled. After I left the job fair, I found that the whole experience was surprising and unexpected. Soon enough the second interview came and went through a third and final interview. Then three weeks later I started my new position. My friends were happy and supportive at the new things that were happening. Things were going well so much so that one of my friends invited me to a dinner party. I went, of course. When good things are happening in your life, always take it and give thanks for the graces and blessings.

The dinner party came and we were there wearing our gorgeous dresses. The people were friendly and well-dressed. It was not a black-tie dinner party, but it was formal. My friend kept motioning to look to my left, telling me that this handsome gentlemen had been eying me since we entered the ballroom and he was walking towards us. Wow! I just didn't have the time to take this in, and I heard this voice behind us. This voice was resonating the greeting as if it were music to our ears. I turned around and greeted him. He introduced himself as Nick and we introduced ourselves *(myself, Loreina, and my friend Catia).*

Catia left us to dance with a friend. Nick and I remained conversing with one another. Nick was very interesting. We hit it off well. I had a good feeling in my heart about him. I found that I can tell Nick anything and he was so good with it. He wasn't a push over, but he was practical and realistic. One of the many qualities I really liked about him. He was also generous and almost doting. I was the same way with him. We would buy gifts for each other when we would return from a trip. Our jobs took us away at times. He was wonderful. My family liked him and he liked them too. Nick became friends with Marja and Harrington. My mom adored him and he the same. During that year and half we came to know each other very well. I also met his family: Maxx, Brandon, and Vera. It was surprising to find out that Nick had a twin brother named Maxx. They were similar in looks accept for their eyes. Maxx had blue eyes and Nick had hazel eyes.

After a year and half of courting and being together, we became engaged. We loved each other so much, we didn't want to wait forever to get married. Nick and I were very traditional in that we didn't live together. Nick knew about my relationship with the Lord and that I preserved myself *(living a chaste life)* out of respect and honor to the Lord. Nick respected that and didn't pressure me. I really loved him for it because not all people were like that. We were practically best friends. Our relationship wasn't perfect, but we always worked on compromising and seeing each other's point-of-view. Nick worked long hours and I did as well. Therefore, there were times when we wouldn't see each other for two weeks at a time. Even though we would miss each other, it was great because we made special plans together. We respected each other at all levels.

We planned our wedding in six months. During that time we did meet with our pastor for pre-marital sessions. This included going on retreats together, which we found to be the highlight of it all. We were able to re-group in a peaceful way with the Lord. We did gain a greater perspective and it brought us closer together in faith. Our love for each seemed to expand and have more meaning. We integrated our ideas and what we liked and how we wanted our wedding to embody. Since the wedding was about us, it made sense for us to be part of the planning process. It wasn't one sided. I don't think our whole time together was ever one-sided. It just seemed to be that way. I think that we knew in our hearts that we were destined to be together and just accepted it. This made it so much easier between us. We also knew that we weren't together because of some social norm, but we were together out of love for each other. This type of bond made our relationship stronger.

Our wedding came. We had the nuptials at our parish and we had the reception at the same ballroom that we first met in. I remember walking down the aisle of our parish in my beautiful white lace gown with a three foot train made with the same lace design. My bouquet was made with pale pink roses with white calla lilies and baby's breath all held together by a long white organza ribbon. Nick was wearing a handsome formal tuxedo that was especially tailored to his fit his medium frame and height. Maxx was standing next to Nick as his best man. Our pastor was standing at the center in front of the altar between us. Everyone we invited RSVP'd and came to our wedding and reception. There were a hundred people at our wedding and reception. We received beautiful and functional gifts, cards with surprises and getaway packages. We were overjoyed. We went on our honeymoon to Oahu, Hawaii. It was a three week honeymoon. When we returned home, we started making plans for our immediate future. In the interim, we took some time and sent *Thank You* cards to all our wedding guests, which included our family. Then we began our plan to purchase a home together. We hired a Realtor to help us find a new home. We found a beautiful home and made our first purchase. It was spacious with high-ceilings and lots of rooms. The home sat on a two-acre lot. It was near our jobs. Nick wanted to take care of the landscaping. I said only if I get to have my vegetable garden. We agreed. We planned on having a lot of children and it made sense to purchase this home. After a year of being married, we decided to start having children.

Well, my journey to motherhood was pretty interesting. The first time I became pregnant we were excited and started making plans for the nursery. Then two-months into the pregnancy, I suffered a miscarriage. We grieved the loss together for a bit and decided to try again. The second time all went well and in nine months I gave birth to our first child, a baby boy in the Spring. We named him Dachon. He was a little beauty resembling his father with those piercingly hazel eyes and curly dark hair. He was a happy baby, and his father was even happier because they resembled each other. Our families spent time with us during the second week celebrating our little treasure. In a few months Dachon had his baptism and ceremony. He grew healthy.

Then, when Dachon was near turning three years old, we decided to have another child. My relationship with the Lord was growing as well. I would spend time in prayer praying for a little girl. Then one day came where I started feeling nauseous and this would happen every morning for one month. I took the test, and it was positive. Then, I went to see the doctor, and she told me that yes I was with child. Bun in the oven. My prayers were answered. We were so happy. Then, three weeks later, on my off day, I felt liquid running through my inner thigh and a sharp pain just below my abdomen. When I looked down, I saw blood running down my inner thigh to the floor collecting in a small pool. I fell down on my knees in utter shock, not knowing what to do. Since we kept a phone in the bathroom, I called my doctor and explained to her what happened. She said that I was having a miscarriage. That I had lost the baby. This happened every two months for eight months. I started asking the Lord why this was happening. The Lord didn't answer my questions. He kept silent. I told Him all the good things I did and how I loved spending time with Him. I thanked the Lord for all He had given me and our family. I thanked Him for our beautiful son, Dachon. I felt consoled by Him. However, I couldn't understand why the miscarriages were happening. Then, finally one day, I surrendered it to the Lord. I said to the Lord, "If it is your will for me to have another child, then You will make it happen." Then, I left the chapel (of the parish that we attended) and didn't think about it again. We stopped trying. My husband was a faithful man and had a sense that the timing for a child was probably not a good one, so he didn't push the issue. The three of us returned to our little bliss for a bit.

The fall season was looming ahead, and we had to get the house ready for it. Every season we prepared the house making changes and adding decorations to celebrate the new season. As a family, to us it was about giving thanks to God for His Creation and allowing us as family to enjoy it while bringing others to enjoy it too. We did volunteer work each season. This season it would be volunteering at the homeless shelter. We didn't do a lot of volunteering because of our time schedules, but we made sacrifices to devote ourselves to one each season. We loved it, and the people were always pleased. Our son, Dachon, loved it because he loved speaking about the Lord to the youngsters, and they listened intently. It was pretty interesting to watch. We always felt a sense of joy. It never went away, and we felt it stronger when we did work like this. We even wanted to open a homeless shelter of our own one day. It was like a family dream. Soon Thanksgiving came. The beautiful thing about this wonderful holiday is that both of our families would come to our home for Thanksgiving weekend. It was so jovial; everyone was getting along and catching up on old times. It was always great! Thanksgiving dinner was something to marvel at only because us women would make a special dish dear to our hearts specific for Thanksgiving dinner. Therefore, this dinner would be hearty and tasteful. To be honest, I think that is why everyone was so joyful, especially after eating Thanksgiving dinner. Weekend shopping was another event we loved; this is when we did our Christmas shopping. Sunday evening arrives, and we are again saying good-bye and wishing Godspeed for the journey.

Next wonderful event was Christmas. For me, personally, and my faith this holiday was a season; and it began on Christmas Eve. My husband always thought that it was strange until he started studying my faith and understood the reason and embraced it. With this new outlook he was at ease. Therefore, we observed Advent and Christmas season. Advent was a time to prepare ourselves for the coming of the Lord. It was not just about preparing our house; it was also about preparing ourselves. We spent personal alone times with the Lord, going to confession and spending family time with the Lord as well. It was wonderful because it was a time we share our hearts and our dreams and how we each felt about the coming of our Lord and what it meant to each of us personally. My main focus was with Mary. I always marveled at the faith of Mary. She was a woman that just believed God. Her relationship with the God was very strong. Most women put getting married first than putting God first. Mary was a different woman. Although she was betrothed to Joseph, she accepted God's invitation without knowing how it was going to turn out or that it would begin before she took her final vows as Joseph's wife. So for me, personally, I loved this time. My husband related more to Joseph. He always defended Joseph, and it was so dear to watch and hear him. Saying that Joseph had the burden of a family to carry Dachon seemed to speak of the baby Jesus saying, "He is real special."

This year Christmas was special because that was the time Evia was conceived, and I didn't know that I was with child until three months of pregnancy. I didn't have the signs of pregnancy: no morning sickness, no crazy appetites, no weight gain, my moods were normal, and my body felt normal. As a matter fact, I felt a strange sense of peace and tranquility during that three-month time.

It was during March when I went for my yearly checkup with my gynecologist where wc made a discovery. He was feeling my abdomen when he had a peculiar look on his face. Then the look vanished and I dismissed it as nothing. After examining me, he went into the other room and came back and gave me a pregnancy test kit. He told me to go in the bathroom. I looked at him like "not this again." He motioned for me to go. I obliged. I came back and gave it to him. He took it and left the examining room. He returned and took the stool and sat down. Dr. Chung said, "Loreina, you are three months pregnant."

I was shocked and asked Dr. Chung, "How can that happen? I haven't had any pregnancy symptoms at all. I even get my menstruations as normal."

Dr. Chung said, "Well, that happens sometimes. We don't know why it happens. The human body is a mystery. We doctors are humbled at these happenings that we cannot explain with laboratory tests or stethoscope. Of course, miracles are not out of the question though. Now, that is something that we cannot rule out." I looked at Dr. Chung and wondered if he was a man of faith. It sounded as if he is.

"You know, Dr. Chung, I think you are right. So what do I do now?" Dr. Chung suggested that I take prenatal vitamins, less stress, less work, no lifting heavy things, eat healthy foods low in cholesterol and low in salt. I made notes of his suggestions and thanked him, and he gave me a prescription for any back pains. (*I suffer from chronic back pain.*) He said that the dosages were low and wouldn't hurt the baby. I smiled, squeezed his hand, and left. Walking to my car in the parking lot, I felt happy yet afraid. It is hard to forget those horrible times of miscarriage, but they were not hurtful memories anymore. I felt a sense of inner strength when I thought about it. Like I survived some sort of battle or something. I touch my womb and thought about the little life growing in there. I drove straight home. I didn't return to work, and my assistant had instructions of what I wanted him to do in case my doctor's appointment took most of the day. So all was well. I went home and started making dinner. My husband Nick was picking up Dachon, so no one was home yet. The house was quiet. I always loved these moments of silence. It was a time for me and my Creator. I rested on the new facts I learned with Dr. Chung today, and that rest brought peace to my heart. This peace I can only share with my Creator and then share with my loved ones. I felt like this moment was so sacred. Like this moment was purposed by something greater than myself. This child was somehow special, yet I know that Dachon was special as well. The phone started ringing taking me away from my sacred thoughts. I walked over and grabbed the phone, "Hello." The bubbling voice on the other end said, "Hi, honey, just finished picking up Dachon, and we are on our way home now." With a smile on my own face, I said, "Okay, honey, I'm preparing dinner and waiting for you guys. I have some wonderful news to share." My husband said, "Love you, 'til later. I can not wait to hear what this wonderful news is." We said our goodbyes and hung-up. Funny, after we disconnected, I had this weird sad feeling inside. I dismissed it as nerves and continued on.

Twist and Turns

I was beginning to get worried. My husband and son hadn't come home yet, and it had been two hours since we had spoken. This was crazy. I called my husband's cell several times and received no answer. Dr. Chung was careful to tell me to not stress myself out. Well, it was beginning to be stressful, and I tried to steer myself by thinking of happy thoughts that they had gone to the store and were waiting in a very long line. Then reason would enter my thoughts and before you know it, my thoughts would wonder to why my husband was not answering his phone.

By this time, dinner was finished and was growing warm. I was pacing for one minute and another minute I was flipping the channels. Then, I heard a knock at the door. It was already evening and I walked up to the window. I looked between the drapes and saw two policemen. My heart was aching a little, but I tried to remain strong thinking of the little one growing in my womb. I opened the door and the two policemen asked in unison, "Can we speak with Mrs. Oberon?"

I looked at them and said, "I am Mrs. Oberon. Can I help you? My husband is on his way. Is there a problem?" They both looked at each other as if something was making them uncomfortable. They asked if they may come in. I motioned them in and we went over to the dining area and sat at the table. The table was set for dining.

Then one began to speak explaining what happened. He explained, "There was a horrible shooting at a nearby gas station, and the criminals had gotten away. This caused a police chase for the capture of the criminals. During the police chase, several cars were involved in a domino-effect car crash. Seven people involved died instantly, and three were flown to the nearest hospital. The three have just come out of surgery and are in critical condition. Your husband and son are two of the three." The whole time the police officer was talking my mind kept flashing back and forth from past to present. It seemed to do it at critical points. When he said that my husband and son were two of the three, my thoughts flashed back to when we were decorating the house for the holidays. Then, my thoughts returned to the present. Here this made me close my eyes and with a lump in my throat and an aching heart. My husband and Dachon were not dead, but they were in critical condition. My thoughts flashed to the seven people that were dead and their families and tears welled up in my eyes for them and this tragedy. At this point, the policemen were saying that they caught the criminals and arrested them. I thought 'thank goodness' for justice. Raising my thoughts heavenward, I asked in the silence of my own thoughts, Dear Lord, why do we have to endure such violence in our world?' I didn't receive an answer right away. However, I knew somehow He would answer this question.

I looked at the two policemen and asked them if my husband and son were at the local hospital. They both nodded. "Yes." I walked to the kitchen and turned off the burner from warm and made a quick pack for dinner. I packed some dinner in a container for the policemen and gave it to them. I thank them for bringing me the news. Then I grabbed my jacket, purse, keys, and we all walked out. Locking the front door behind me, they asked me if I needed them to escort me to the hospital, I nodded 'yes', just in case. They escorted me. When I reached the hospital, I thanked the policemen for escorting me and walked over to the lobby desk. I told them why I was there and showed them my ID. They had me fill out a short form and gave me a visitor's pass. My husband and Dachon were in the same room and on the twelfth floor. In the elevator, I felt so warm, and for the first time, I felt movement in my womb. I felt the baby moving. It gave me a warm feeling inside. I finally reached the twelfth floor and walked up the nurses' station. Again, I introduced myself, showing them the visitor's pass. I asked them for my husband and son's room. They told me, and one nurse showed me where they were staying. As we walked down the hallway, I noticed that this was the intensive care unit (ICU). We reached their room. We gently and quietly walked in. They were both sleeping. I asked the nurse if they had awakened since the surgeries. She had said 'no'. Then all of a sudden, I felt like going to the bathroom asked her where the bathroom was. She pointed to the right. The bathroom was inside the hospital room. I walked in and used the bathroom. While using the bathroom, I felt something was wrong. I was like, "Oh no, not another miscarriage." I inched up and looked in the bowl and saw the water was clear yellow. Feeling strange, I quickly wiped, pulled myself together, washed my hands, and walked out. I still felt strange. Then I felt a sharp pain in my womb, and thank goodness the nurse was still in the room checking on Nick and Dachon. She saw the wincing look on my face and asked what was wrong. I said to her that I didn't feel well and told her that I was three months pregnant, nearing four months, and I had found out earlier that day. She said she would find a doctor to come and take a look at me. I said okay. Still in pain, wincing, I walked over to Dachon. I looked at him. He was just four years old and small with IVs attached to him. I held his little hands and kissed his forehead. Then walked over to my husband's bed and saw the same thing: IVs and his big form lying almost lifeless and his dark curly hair. I glanced at the both of them, so identical. By this time, the pain was getting worse; and as soon as I began to wonder where the nurse had gone, I felt a hand on my shoulder saying, "Mrs. Oberon?" I turned around and saw the doctor looking back at me. Asking me if I was all right.

I said, "No, I'm in a lot of pain right now. I just found out today that I am pregnant and that my husband and son were involved in a horrible accident. I don't want to have another miscarriage. Can you please check me?"

He looked at me and nodded. I went with the doctor. He took me to an examination room. He asked me to lie down on the examining table. I obliged. He asked me where the pain was exactly; I told him in my womb. He asked me if I had gone to the bathroom. I said yes. He asked me if I was spotting blood or if there was blood in the water. I said no to both questions. He said that they were going to check on the baby to see what is going on and why I was in so much pain.

The doctor came back with a sonogram technician with the machine. The technician was a young woman. She reminded me of my sister who was in the same field as well. I started to think about my sister and how I wish she was here with me. Anyway, back to reality. The sonogram technician was wiping this gel on my abdomen area below my navel while the machine was setting up itself. When the machine was ready, it beeped. She started rolling the device over my abdomen. She was explaining to me that they were trying to get a visual of the baby. After a few minutes, they started seeing the baby. The doctor was looking very closely at the visuals and couldn't believe what he was seeing. It looked as if the baby was trying to move toward the birth canal as he was saying to us. The doctor also noticed that the baby was a girl. From what the he was telling it seemed that she wanted to be born. I noticed that the doctor had an astonished expression on his face, I asked him, "Doctor, is there something wrong with the baby?"

The doctor turned around to look at me and said, "It looks like you have a baby girl, and it seems like she wants to come out early."

I asked him, "How can it be when she is only almost four months old? What are you going to do?"

The doctor sat down and looked at me saying, "We have to keep you here to watch over you and the little babe. I'm going to ask the nurse to prepare a room for you here and have them take care of your admittance paperwork. In the meantime, we will find out how your husband and son are doing. By the way, I want to formerly introduce myself. I am Dr. Waverly, I'm an obstetrician/gynecologist. The little babes and their moms are my specialty." He had a little grin on his face when he said it.

I said, with a half a smile, "So I'm going to have a baby girl. I've been praying for a girl. I'm still so worried about my husband and son. I have an obstetrician/gynecologist, his name is Dr. Chung. He prescribed low stress, and this day has been nothing but stress. You see, I have a history of miscarriages, so he gave me some specifics. Therefore, I understand. I'll oblige. Can you call Dr. Chung and let him know for me?" Dr. Waverly nodded and put his hand in mine and gently squeezed it and left saying he would be back.

I was still in pain, but they have gone down a little. Dr. Waverly returned to the examining room. He said, "I called Dr. Chung, and he wants me to keep you in the hospital for a couple of days. He said that he will be in tomorrow morning to check in with you." I felt a sense of relief. However, I was still worried about my husband, Nick, and Dachon. It had been hours since they came out of surgery, and they were still sleeping. I hadn't spoken to the doctor to find out the details. I didn't even know what they had surgery on. Dachon's head was wrapped with bandages and Nick's head was also wrapped with bandages. Dachon's left leg and right arm were in a cast. Those were the extent of the injuries that were visible when I was in their room that brief moment. My heart was aching. I don't know what the outcome will be and if they will live through this. I'm afraid of losing them. They are my heart. If they are gone, a part of me would be gone too. It would be devastating. Not being able to think about it anymore, I pushed the thoughts away from my mind. Dr. Waverly had left to prepare a room for me. I tried to ask him if he can place me in a room next to Nick and Dachon or at least on the same floor. He said that he would try. I'm hoping that he can. I couldn't take it anymore, so I text and called my sister and mom to tell them what happened. They were both devastated. My sister said she would drive down and would be there next morning. My mom said that she would be here as soon as she could. She was out of town on business and on a mission trip. I tried to tell her not to come, but she insisted. I called Harrington, my brother, to let him know what happened. "Hi, Harrington, this is Loreina. How are you, my dear brother?" Before he could answer, my voice broke. "Harrington, Nick and Dachon were in a car accident several hours ago and have just come out of surgery. To top it all off, I found out earlier that I've been pregnant for over three months. Nick doesn't know yet. Harrington, I'm totally scared. I know that the Lord is watching over them regardless of what happens, but I want them to come out of this okay. There is no telling now. Only in time, you know?" Harrington was silent and devastated. He had known Nick since before we were married and had really grown fond of him like a brother. He remembered the times with Nick and Maxx having their "boy's night out times" and discussions about how their lives had come together and how they helped each other. Now this.

Harrington was thinking, *Wow, how life just turns. I have to try to be strong for Loreina.* Harrington reassured Loreina, "I'm sure Nick and Dachon will come out fine. Nick is strong and Dachon, my little nephew tiger, will pull through. Keep thinking that. How are you and the baby?"

I just didn't want to talk anymore, but Harrington sounded so concerned. "I am not too good, and the baby may be in distress. I am trying to stay strong, but my worst fears seem to keep coming up. I'll try to be strong. In the meantime, the doctor wants to observe me overnight because of the pains I'm having near my lower abdomen. He said that it's routine to keep an eye on the baby. I also called Mom and Marja. There's Nick's family to contact."

Harrington, hearing the weariness in my voice, volunteered to contact Nick's family. Harrington remembered them during family gatherings me and Nick would have each year. "Loreina, I will contact them for you. Don't worry about it."

Loreina, feeling like it is her responsibility, wanted to decline but didn't want to talk with anyone right now. Harrington's suggestion was probably a blessing in disguise. "Okay, Harrington. You can call Nick's family." Harrington, knowing Maxx, more decided to call him first.

Harrington lived out of town. He, Nick, and Maxx were very good guy friends. They all met at family gatherings me and Nick and Nick's parents would have each year. He and Nick are good friends and had often worked together on Harrington's projects. Harrington was still shocked at the news. Harrington knew that Nick and Loreina had wanted to have a girl. He also knew that Nick liked being a father. Harrington himself did not have his own children; however, he started a ministry for boys that didn't have father figures in their lives. Therefore, he and Nick connected a lot with each other because of certain situations that may arise, and he would need Nick's advice. Nick had visited

Chicos, Harrington's ministry, and was really impressed with how the boys were responding to him. Harrington knew how impressed Nick and Maxx really were with his work. Since Harrington knew Maxx to be down-to-earth like his brother Nick, he invited Maxx to teach art to the youth. At that time, Maxx was looking to work with the youth, and the opportunity was a blessing. Maxx had been to Chico's Ministry and was teaching a class called the Art You Feel. This class helped the boys visualize their life by painting it on canvas. They had to create from a place of emotion. It was their chance to express themselves in the raw. Harrington was impressed with the idea, knowing that it would be a good step for the boys to take in getting in touch with their emotional side. The class became a source of healing for them. Maxx really connected with them, and they connected with Maxx. Harrington remembered how he himself felt so lost without a father figure in his life. The dark moments he had growing up without a dad and having to cope with that. He remembered the pain.

Now he had to call Maxx with this devastating news. It was just a difficult task, but it had to be done. Harrington looked at his cell phone and started dialing Maxx's phone number. The phone rang, and after the third ring, Maxx answered, "Hello?"

Harrington took a deep breath and closed his eyes. "Hello, Maxx, this is Harrington. How are you? Are you busy?"

Maxx replied, "Hey, Harrington, how are you? I'm doing fine. No, I'm not busy now, just finished my work for the evening. Why? Is everything alright? You don't sound to well." Maxx sensed something was wrong.

Harrington was trying to find the words to tell Maxx about what happened to Nick and Dachon. "Loreina called me earlier and told me that Nick and Dachon were involved in an accident. There were three survivors, and they were two of the three. They were flown to the local hospital for emergency surgery. Now they are in the ICU recovering. Loreina is not doing well herself. She just found out earlier today that she is three months pregnant. The doctor has admitted her to the hospital to watch her and the baby. The shock of it all has caused some major pains below her abdomen. Loreina wanted me to tell you and the family, but she's not able to and asked me to call you, Brandon, and Vera. Maxx, can you share the news with the rest of the family? Both Nick and Dachon are in critical condition, and the doctors are watching them closely."

Maxx is standing there at his home holding the cell phone in his hand while listening to what Harrington is saying. He is trying to take it all in, yet a feeling of numbness seems to take over. He cannot respond to Harrington. He remembered that he was just talking to Nick that morning, and had this weird feeling inside during that time. Following that feeling, he told his brother how much he loved him and now this. Coming back to the present and finding the words, Maxx said, "Harrington, thank you for telling me. I can't believe…Wow! I just spoke to Nick this morning. He sounded fine. Loreina must be devastated and with her being pregnant. She can't be well right now. I can't imagine Nick and Dachon in this critical state. Dear God! I will call mom and dad to let them know. What are you going to do, Harrington? I am going to see if I can take the next flight out to be with them."

Harrington said, "I'm going to do the same. Take the next flight out to be with Loreina, Nick, Dachon, and the baby. I know Mom and Marja are on their way there. Wow, Maxx. I can't believe it. They will pull through this. I know it! We just have to keep them in our prayers. Well, I'll see you there. Let me know if there is anything I can do for you."

Maxx answered, "I will see you at the hospital later. Thank you, Harrington, for calling me. I appreciate it. I will see you later. I'm going to call Mom and Dad. I'll talk to you soon. Bye!"

Harrington said, "Okay, bye, Maxx. Talk to you soon!" They both hung up. Harrington was still devastated. He moved over to the computer and started looking for the nearest flight to the west coast of Florida where Loreina and Nick reside.

Tragic Situations

Morning came and Mom and Marja had made it to the hospital. I woke up in tears, and Marja was there to comfort me. I couldn't sleep thinking that Nick and Dachon were a few doors away from mine and in critical condition. Harrington had called earlier that morning to let me know that he had contacted Maxx to tell him the news. He said Maxx was going to let Nick's parents, Brandon and Vera, know what happened. Harrington said he was able to get a flight out as early as this afternoon and would come straight to the hospital. I told him Mom and Marja were here with me. Maxx called shortly after Harrington. He didn't sound too good but was trying to be optimistic saying that Nick and Dachon would pull out of it. Maxx said he found an early flight and would be there early afternoon. His parents were coming later in the evening. I told him that we would be waiting for him and them. I thanked Maxx for telling Brandon and Vera about what happened. He said it was not a problem; we are one big family. It was warming to hear him say that. He asked me how I was doing. I told him not too well but staying strong. I told Maxx that I was pregnant with a baby girl. He was happy of the news that he was going to be an uncle to a niece. However, it was bittersweet since his brother and nephew were hanging on to life right now. Maxx and I said our goodbyes and that we would see him soon.

Mom came in the room with some breakfast. I couldn't eat now, but she reminded me that I was eating for two, and I needed to be strong to go see Nick and Dachon. I knew she was right. I ate as much as possible. I told them that Harrington and Maxx were on their way. They were pleased to hear this news. Mom and Marja were prepping me to go see Nick and Dachon. Deep down inside I was afraid to visit them. Not for nothing, but they were my heart. I cherished them as God's gift to me. It seemed that I had to give this gift back. *Lord, I didn't want to give them back.*

Mom and Marja took me to see Nick and Dachon. When we arrived in their hospital room, they were both in the same way as I had left them. Nick's head was wrapped in bandages. Dachon's right leg and left arm were in a cast. Dachon's head was still wrapped in bandages. I walked over to Nick and squeezed his hand. I kissed him on his forehead. I just kept thinking of how much we loved each other. Tears were welling up in my eyes. I still couldn't believe that this was happening. I looked over at Dachon, got up from Nick's bed, and walked over to him. I kissed him on the forehead and held his little hands in mine. I remember the times where I would rock him to sleep while telling him little bedtime stories. He would fall asleep in my arms, and now he lay there helpless; there was nothing I can do, but pray that the Lord would bring them back to me. I tried to think positively and with optimism. This wasn't easy. I stayed with them through lunch. They still hadn't awakened yet. When the doctor came to see them, I asked the doctor if this was normal for them to not awaken for this long since their surgery. He said yes. He said recovery can take months and sometimes a patient can lapse into a coma. He said that they were not in a coma, but in a sleeping state.

Afternoon came and Maxx had made it to the hospital. Harrington and Nick's parents were on their way. Mom and Marja filled Maxx in on what was happening, which was not much. Maxx came into their room. We greeted each other and hugged. Then he moved over to Nick and kissed him on the forehead. He held Nick's hand. For a brief moment, I thought Nick's hand moved a bit. Maxx saw his little nephew, Dachon, on the other bed. He replaced Nick's hand and walked over to his nephew and kissed him on the forehead. He held Dachon's little hand in his. It was a moment of nostalgia. Indescribable. Our hearts lay on the two beds and, at that moment, time was not ours. We were not in control. Their life hangs at the hands of fate and with faith standing on the background of hope.

I couldn't take it anymore. The hospital had a chapel. I went there to sit with the Lord. What else can I do? I knelt and stared at the Risen Lord image over the altar. I prayed to my Risen Lord and asked him if my Nick and Dachon that He gave me as a gift can rise too. I prayed with an aching heart that His will would be done, whichever way it went; I gave thanks to my Risen Lord that I was able to have happy memories with them. I prayed that whichever way it goes that the babe in my womb would be safe, and I thanked the Lord for this little gift of life as well. I gave my Risen Lord my sorrows, my pain and my aching heart. I told Him that in the silence of my faith, I am sad that this happened, and I know somehow all things would work for the greater good. I thanked the Lord for this sense of strength I still feel within. The pains in my lower abdomen were not as bad as before. The pain had subsided. I just sat there in silence. Helpless, but not really. I looked up at the image of my Lord, and with raw heartfelt pleas, I prayed, "Lord, I don't want them to go to heaven yet. I want us to spend more time together. Dachon is only four. Nick loves his community projects. We have our family dream to fulfill. I know heaven is a better place. I just want some more time with them. We love them. In all this, I respect Your will." I knelt before the Lord and said the Lord's Prayer and the Hail Mary and genuflected. I left the chapel and returned to their room.

By this time, Nick's parents and Harrington were in Nick and Dachon's room. I hugged them all and told them I was spending some quiet time at the chapel. Nick's father, Brandon, was sitting with Nick; and Nick's mom, Vera, was sitting with Dachon. They were silent. I left Brandon and Vera alone with Nick and Dachon and went to the lobby to be with the others. On the way to the lobby, I felt a sharp excruciating pain in my lower abdomen. I nearly fell on the floor. Thank goodness a nurse was walking by and held me up. There was a wheelchair that was stationed on the side of the wall of the hallway. She wheeled it over to me and helped me to sit on it. She asked me if I had a room in the hospital. I told her yes and that my family was in the lobby. She wheeled me to the lobby. Harrington came forward, and the nurse told him that I needed to rest because I nearly collapsed in the hallway. Mom, Marja, Maxx, and Harrington took me to my room. They said that they would check on Nick and Dachon for me. What could I say? I needed to rest because if I didn't the little baby in my womb would be in danger. I could go to see Nick and Dachon a little later. I rested for about two hours and woke up feeling better. Nick's parents were in my room. "Hi, Brandon and Vera. How are you? Were there any responses from Nick and Dachon?" I asked.

Brandon said, "They both have not awakened yet. I did feel Nick squeezing my thumb a little, but Dachon has been the same." Vera was solemn. She smiled at me a little. I could see the worry on her face. I sat up from the bed and reached over to touch her hand. "We just have to stay strong and hope for the best." She nodded yes. Brandon asked what happened. I motioned them to sit down and proceeded to explain to them what happened. I started from what the police officers informed me about the car chase that led multiple car accident to the three people being air lifted to the nearest hospital for emergency surgeries. They both sat there in dismay. I told them that Nick hadn't found out yet that I was pregnant with our child (tears welling up in eyes). They nodded with understanding. Brandon and Vera got up and came over to me. We hugged with a sense of reassurance. I said, "Let us go see Nick and Dachon." The pain had subsided, and I was able to sit on the wheelchair without help. They wheeled me to Nick and Dachon's room.

While we were there, the nurse came and announced that visiting hours would be over in thirty minutes. I told everyone that they would stay at our house. Mom and Marja were in charge of making sure everyone was settled there for their stay. They both new our house very well, so I knew everyone would be okay. Everyone started to say their good-byes to Nick and Dachon. I myself was wheeled back into my room with instructions that Dr. Chung and Dr. Waverly would be there to check up on me. The nurse in charge of Nick and Dachon said that Dr. Friedman *(he performed the surgeries on Nick)* would be in tomorrow morning to check on Nick, and Dr. Waverly would also check on Dachon in the morning as well. I said okay. I just felt like I was at a standstill with nothing to do. You know at this point there really was nothing to do, but be patient and continue visiting them. Everything was in the Lord's hands now. The Lord was giving me strength and peace from within. I gave thanks to Lord and prayed that both Nick and Dachon would pull through with God's grace. With these thoughts in mind, I fell asleep.

Next morning, I woke up early around 5:00 a.m. The hospital room was quiet. I decided to get ready and go visit Nick and Dachon. I miss spending alone time with them. I have not heard from anyone yet. The pains in my lower abdomen had subsided. I didn't feel them and it was a relief, because I was able to freshen up with no problem. Feeling stronger, I didn't use the wheelchair and walked down to the opposite side of the twelfth floor to the ICU area. The hallway was very quiet. The nurses' station was also quiet. The energy was quiet and serene. At this point, it didn't feel like this was a hospital, which seemed odd for me to think that. As I turned the corner, the scenery changed before me, I saw nurses and doctors coming in and out of Nick and Dachon's hospital room. Here, there was a lot of energy in the area at such an early morning. Approaching their room, I stopped one of the nurses. She recognized me and said, "Oh, Mrs. Oberon, we were just about to come and see you. Mr. Oberon and your son, Dachon, are in distress. We are trying to stabilize them. The doctors are inside doing the best they can to stabilize them."

I said, "Okay, what happened to make them go into distress?"

The nurse, looking at them and me, said, "It is complications from their surgeries. They lost a lot of blood during surgery, and both of them had to receive two pints of blood each. The loss of blood weakened them, but the blood transfusion would have made them stronger by now."

I finally asked the direct question, "I see that they had bandages wrapped around their head. What exactly was the surgery that they had undergone?"

The nurse sat me down and explained the procedure in brevity. She explained, "They both suffered brain injuries that caused hemorrhaging. The doctors had to perform surgeries to stop the hemorrhaging and swelling. After twenty-four hours of rest from surgery, the swelling went down a bit, but the distress is most likely coming from any clot that has formed. The doctors are giving them medications through IVs, and this should dissolve any blood clots that are forming."

I listened intently and asked her another hard question *(It was hard for me not necessarily hard for them. I was cringing inside when I asked her the question)*, "What will happen if the blood clots do not dissolve?" The nurse looked at me and said that she would have Dr. Friedman explain it more to me, but right now, she had to get back to assisting the doctors. What could I say but okay? I just had to wait for Dr. Friedman to finish stabilizing them and let me know more details. In the meantime, I had to call Mom and Marja to have everyone come to the hospital because of the turn of events. I phoned the house, and it was Mom who picked up the phone.

"Hi, Mom, how are you?"

Mom said, "I couldn't sleep during the night, thinking about Nick and Dachon." I could hear my mom was a little worried.

I said, "Well, Mom, rightly so. There has been a turn of events. Nick and Dachon are currently in distress. The doctors are trying to stabilize them by giving them medication to stop the blood clots from forming around the head wounds. Can you tell everyone for me and tell them visiting hours just started?"

My mom was silent for a minute. She said, "Okay, Loreina, I will get everyone to the hospital. How are you? Did you sleep well during the night?"

I answered my mom, "Not really, I slept, but I was sleeping from weariness and from being tired. I woke up at 5:00 a.m. and wanted to go spend some alone time with Nick and Dachon. When I reached their room, there were two nurses and two doctors going in and out of their room. Then the nurse told me that they were in distress. Well, I'm waiting for all of you to get here. I can't talk anymore. Mom, I will see all of you soon."

Mom said, "Hang in there, Loreina, we will be there as soon we can, okay?"

I mumbled, "Okay. Bye for now. Love all of you. See you later." Mom said her good-byes too and said that everyone would be there at the hospital within the hour. I hung up from Mom. By that time, I saw Dr. Friedman and Dr. Waverly walking toward me. They did not look too good. I was thinking to myself, *What now? Enough is enough already.* I knew inside that the way they were walking and looking that things were amiss. I said a small prayer for the Lord's strength with tears welling up in my eyes. Before Dr. Friedman and Dr. Waverly could sit with me, I wiped the tears from my eyes. I needed to be strong to hear what they had to say, good or bad. I walked over the nearest lobby close to Nick and Dachon's room and sat down. They sat down next to me.

Dr. Friedman started first, "Mrs. Oberon, things are not looking good for Nick and Dachon. Have you spoken to the family yet?" I just looked at him, and at that moment, I had a flashback of Nick, Dachon, and me at the park two months ago having the time of our lives chasing each other, playing hide-and-seek and peek-a-boo, just laughing our heads off; and at the end of the day, my little Dachon hugged and kissed us both and told us how much he loved us. We just hugged him back and told him that we loved him too. I blinked my eyes to fight back the tears. Coming back to reality, I answered Dr. Friedman, "Yes, they are on the way. Everyone should be here soon. You want to wait until everyone is here to say the details, or do you want to talk now?"

They both looked at each other, and Dr. Waverly said, "No. They are both diminishing. During the surgery your husband and son lost a lot of blood, therefore we issued blood transfusions to replenish the loss. Right now they are suffering distress because of the blood clots that are forming at a rapid rate. The blood clots are hindering their recovery. We are giving them medications to control the blood clots, but these same medications have major side effects. Therefore, we have lowered the dosages. The flip side is that these dosages are not high enough to stop the blood clots quickly enough. The brain swelling has gone down tremendously since the surgery."

Listening and thinking through what they were saying made me realize that Nick and Dachon were fighting for their lives. The thought of them not making it through this fight was something that I don't want to think about. I looked at both doctors and said, "Now, they have a new battle. Is that what you are saying?"

They both answered, "Yes."

I said, "So what solutions do you have? We have to wait and see. This is where we are at right now?"

Dr. Friedman answered, "The solution is to keep giving them the medications to lower the blood clots. We just don't know if they are going to make it through because of their strength level. The accident they were in was very traumatic to their system. When they were in surgery, they both were almost near flat-lining because their blood pressures were decreasing at a steady rate. We were able to stabilize them through it. At this point, we have to prepare ourselves for the worst while doing our best."

I understood what Dr. Friedman was saying. He was right. There's a big part of me that wanted to walk away from these doctors, go to my husband and son, and hug them close and tell that I loved them and that they were going to get better and I was going to be here for them every step of their recovery. Just then, I realized that time is precious and them telling me this, was a wakeup call to spend time with them while the doctors do their best to make them well *(or not)*. I stood up and thanked the doctors for the news and updates on Nick and Dachon's health recovery. I told them, "Thank you, Dr. Friedman and Dr. Waverly, I appreciate everything that you are doing to help my husband and son recover. I'm going to spend some time with them now."

Dr. Waverly nodded his head in understanding, then he asked me, "Mrs. Oberon have you been having more pain in your lower abdomen?"

I answered, "No, the pains have gone down. Thank you for asking. Well, gentlemen, I'm going to spend time with my two precious people. My family is coming, and I am going to call you when they arrive." I got up and hugged the doctors. The doctors said their good-byes and said that they would return when my family arrived. I left.

Nick and Dachon's room was quiet by now. The nurses and doctors have stabilized them; however, they were not out of the woods yet. I walked over to Nick's bed and took his hands in mine. His hand twitched in mine. Right then and there, it came to me to find out if there was a chaplain assigned to the hospital. I left their room and went to the nurses' station. I asked them, "Do you have a chaplain at this hospital?"

A nurse answered, "Yes, we do. Do you want me to call him for you?"

I answered, "Yes. Do you know if he can come see my husband and son today?"

The nurse said, "I will call him to check. He hasn't come in yet for his rounds, and today is usually his low patient day. Let me call him right now. Wait here." I stood there while the nurse at the desk found his number and called him. Sounds like she was able to reach him.

"Father Charlie, I have someone here asking for a chaplain. Her name is Mrs. Oberon and her husband and son are in ICU. Can you visit their room this morning? I will have her complete the form. You will? Oh, that would be great. Is there a time? 11:00 a.m. All right, we will be waiting for you. God bless, too. Bye!" This was definitely good news that he would be able to visit them. This was important, and our families would be here when he comes.

The nurse gave me a form to complete. It was mainly about our faith and our relationship with the Lord. Nick and I were close to the Lord and practiced the sacraments of the church. We also belonged to a ministry in the church, which reminded me that I had to contact our ministry leader. I gave the nurse the completed form, thanked her for making the arrangements, and returned to Nick and Dachon's room.

I was with them for a few minutes when I heard footsteps in the hallway coming toward the room. If you didn't know it, the family had finally arrived. We all hugged. I asked everyone how they slept. Everyone said so-so. Maxx and Harrington looked really tired. My mom, Marja, Brandon, and Vera looked a little tired. I figured no one slept well. Mom brought me some breakfast and coffee. I had not thought of food at all this morning. I briefed everyone on the happenings that morning. Also, let them know that the chaplain for the hospital, Fr. Charlie, was coming to visit. They were pleased to hear this. Everyone's faith were at different levels; however, they knew that having a relationship with the Lord was a good thing. I let everyone visit with Nick and Dachon while I went on to eat my breakfast at my room before the chaplain arrived.

It was almost forty-five minutes; breakfast was over for me. Mom and Marja came looking for me. They said that the chaplain was in the room and had just arrived. I said a small prayer of thanks to the Lord for this. We returned to the room. I introduced myself to Fr. Charlie. He explained to us what the prayer would be and that they would be receiving the sacrament, anointing of the sick. He explained what it is and that all would be in the Lord's hands. I said to Father Charlie, "I am glad that you are doing this for us." He nodded as if to say that it's all okay. The ceremony was private, and the whole family was there to partake in it. It was a blessing, and afterwards, there was sense of peace among us. Nick's parents, Brandon and Vera, seemed calmer as if they were content. I think we all felt that way. Father Charlie said a blessing over all of us, and we hugged him good-bye.

It's a good thing that they received the special blessing because they both went into distress three hours later. The nurses and the doctors came; this time, there was no reviving Nick and Dachon. They both passed away during that time. We were all in the lobby when Dr. Waverly and Dr. Friedman came to give us the news. Vera and I just sat down on the sofa. We both started weeping. All I could feel is this pain in my heart that I couldn't take away. Everyone else—Brandon, Maxx, Harrington, Mom, and Marja— were saddened. Then a nurse came to visit us. She was the nurse keeping watch over Nick and Dachon. She said that last night Nick had awakened briefly and was asking for me before he went into distress the first time. She said that when it happened again, Dachon had awakened briefly saying, "Mommy, mommy." Then he went into distress; and at that moment, other nurses came and the doctors came to stabilize and revive them. Dr. Friedman did explain to us what happened; therefore, we were hearing this a second time. He mentioned that he tried to bring him to consciousness, but Nick had already gone. Dr. Waverly, being a pediatrician, was with Dachon when he went into distress. He was trying to revive him, but it was too late. Sitting on the sofa with Vera, I began to feel the rush of grief come over me. I felt a deep pain in my soul and a deep pain in my heart. My heart ached. My throat constricted, so I couldn't talk. I started crying, and the pain below my abdomen returned, and Harrington took me to my room to rest. Maxx and Brandon were comforting Vera. Marja came with Harrington. Mom stayed with Vera. I cried all night. My whole body was writhing in grief. It was this grief that would last for weeks. All I keep thinking was how Nick and Dachon were my heart. I felt like without them life was just a blur. The only time I slept was when I was tired of grieving. There were breaking moments of numbness.

The next morning came, and Dr. Waverly came to check on me. The nurse had informed him that the pains had returned. He said the stress was not helping the baby, and I may have to deliver her early. I told him to do whatever he could to keep the baby alive. Especially now. If it meant early delivery, then let it be. I could not control the grief that I felt, but at the same time, I didn't want the baby to suffer. I prayed to the Lord to take control of the life of the baby. I prayed to the Lord to take control of my own life. I asked the Lord why He took Nick and Dachon so soon. I didn't get a chance to tell Nick that I was pregnant with our baby girl. I asked the Lord why. I didn't understand. I didn't understand. My whole being was aching in one way and then numb in another. Then, the grieving started again when I think of Nick's smile and voice. The flood of tears start coming down my cheeks when I think of how Dachon looks like his father—the curly hair, the light brown eyes, pink full lips, thick lashes, and beautiful smile that reveal pearly white straight teeth and when he would climb up on my shoulders and put his little hands around my neck in a hug. These memories would just flood my mind and my whole body would convulse with grief. This time, I felt a sharp pain in my womb and was afraid for the baby all over again. By this time, the nurse came in to check on me. Her name was Nurse Sweetie. She saw me convulsing with grief and rushed to sit next to me and hugged me close to her. This helped me to calm down. I felt consoled, and the pain in my womb subsided. I asked her to call Dr. Waverly and Dr. Chung. I told her that I wanted to speak with them about delivering the baby. The fear of losing the baby was growing, and I couldn't deal with another loss. I can't control the grief, and I know the stress was hurting the baby. Nurse Sweetie, said, "Sure, Mrs. Oberon, I will call both doctors for you. Will you be okay while I'm gone? I can send a bereavement nurse to sit with you. Would you like that?" I nodded. Meanwhile, Marja and Maxx were with me in the room. They sat with me and reassured me to take it easy for the baby. Maxx was also telling me that their parents, Brandon and Vera, were taking care of all funeral arrangements for Nick and Dachon. I totally approved of it and appreciated that they were doing this. At the state I was in right now, I wouldn't be able to handle it. I also let Maxx know that our home would be the place to have reception after the funeral mass. He nodded yes. I was pleased. Maxx and I hugged. He left to let them know and sent Harrington to be with me. Marja was there with me and holding my hand. Marja said, "Bye, Maxx, we will see you later." As Maxx was leaving the room, the bereavement nurse came and introduced herself as Simi. Marja and I nodded and said, "Hi."

Simi looked at the patient and felt so much empathy for her. She sensed that the patient's grief was strong, that she knew that this patient's loss was a deep one. Strong grief can hurt the baby growing in her womb. The baby can go in distress and if that happens, then an emergency C-section would have to be performed to save the baby. Simi moved toward the patient and sat next to her to speak with her. She started to introduce herself and said, "Nurse Sweetie sent me here to spend some time with you. I'm a bereavement nurse specializing in patients that are grieving over loss of a loved one, friends, or someone close to them. As bereavement nurse, I'm able to check their vital signs and make sure the grieving process does not affect their overall condition. Grief can be so severe that it endangers the person's recovery if there's surgery involved or in your case the baby you are carrying. I'm so sorry for your loss, and I'm here to help you get through it while still keeping the little one in there intact. How are you, Loreina?"

It was nice that she addressed me by name. Working at the hospital, sometimes nurses can be so detached, and they seldom use your first name. (It's a kind of protocol professionalism that is detached.) I mean, I understand why. It's just nice to see these two nurses that I've met are really compassionate and not so detached. It's refreshing. Sometimes we have to allow ourselves to be human. I answered, "I'm doing okay. I'm very worried about the baby. I'm sure you've heard everything. It's been hard because you can't control your grief, and at the same time, I don't want to lose the baby. She is so precious."

Simi listened, nodded, and said, "I understand. Nurse Sweetie didn't really tell me much. Just that you are suffering from grief and need a bereavement nurse. I obliged of course. At the hospital, we don't give each other too much information about a patient because we want it to come from the patient. If the patient cannot speak, we check the patient's status chart. It depends on the situation. We gauge each situation separately and go with a need-to-know basis. It helps keep patient confidentiality intact. Also, everything is written on your chart, therefore, it makes it easier. You can share with me at any time. Sharing allows you to empty out and helps you to heal and cope with loss. I want to ask you a few questions about your grief and describe what you are feeling during your grieving moments."

Nurse Simi was interesting, and I like that she explained everything to put me at ease and made me feel comfortable. I didn't want to start grieving crazy again, so I just tried to keep it simple. I told her, "My husband and son were involved in a car collision accident, and three people were airlifted to this hospital for emergency surgery. My husband and son both had suffered head wounds, and my son suffered a broken arm and leg. The third person was also injured severely, causing major trauma to the interior organs. After surgery they were put in ICU to recover. After a few days in recovery, they began to go in distress. The doctors were able to stabilize them the first time, but the second time, it was not successful. They both passed away. The third person is still alive in recovery fighting for his life. I am here because the news of what happened and their passing was such a blow that I began having these major pains in my lower abdomen. The doctor thinks that these may endanger the baby. When I think about them, I grieve uncontrollably for a good long moment. My heart aches, and the ache reaches the depth of me. I feel my soul aching. The grief subsides when someone consoles me. The grief comes and goes. I don't know what to do but to go through it."

At this time, Simi starts taking notes as I described the grief. "I loved my husband and son so deeply. Nick loved me so unconditionally, and we had a special bond connection. He was my soul mate. I mean we always had this deep connection that I can't explain. So losing my hearts—" I stopped. Tears welled up in my eyes. Simi touched my hand for support and I was able to fend off the tears to continue. "When I grieve, my whole being convulses. My heart and soul ache with pain. The emotional pain is so strong. Then I feel this sharp pain in my lower abdomen near the baby. Dr. Waverly did an ultrasound and saw that the baby is near the cervix as if turning into birthing position. So he admitted me here to keep watch over me and the baby. I have told Dr. Waverly to contact my ob/gyn, Dr. Chung. He is supposed to visit me today." We sat talking a little bit. Harrington and Mom came in to check on me. We introduced them to Simi. Mom said she was going to see about getting some dinner for me. I asked her about Brandon and Vera. Harrington said, "They are grieving in a terrible way. Maxx was consoling Vera, and I was consoling Brandon. This is so unexpected. I can't believe that they are gone." I reached over and hugged my brother consoling him. I knew all too well what he meant. I think we all did. We felt it. My heart goes out to all of us, especially Brandon and Vera. I wish I was with them now to console them, but I'm glad that Maxx was with them.

Grief is Upon Us,
Amidst a Little Miracle

My in-laws and my family were taking care of the funeral arrangements. I was involved as well, but they kept me in check to make sure I didn't overdue it. So I made arrangements for funeral mass at the church Nick and Dachon and I attended. It was hard, but I also knew that it was hard for everyone too. I would have bouts of grief and had to just stop through it to regain my strength. A part of me didn't want to do it but knew it had to be done. Nurse Simi came two visit me twice per day—once in the evening and once during the day. She stayed about three hours each time. It's funny because the times she came no one was with me.

One day, during one of the visits with Simi, I felt a sharp pain in my womb. This one was more severe than the other ones. Simi called Dr. Waverly and Dr. Chung right away. Both doctors came, and Dr. Chung started to examine me, and he said that we would have to do an emergency C-section. He said the baby may be in distress and caused the major pains in my lower abdomen. He said the more severe the pains are *(and they have not stopped at all)*, the chances of the baby being born premature are higher. He said that he was going to give me some medication that would help calm the pain for now. However, he informed us that we had to consider this option, that emergency C-section might be in the immediate future. I listened and just went with what they were saying. If the baby is born prematurely then this procedure would be the alternative to keeping her safe. I don't want to lose my precious little gem. I don't know if I can handle another loss. The Lord doesn't give you more than you can handle; if it's becoming too hard, I know His ever loving grace covers you. So I know the best thing we have to do is have the C-section. I looked at Dr. Chung and said, "I agree to the emergency C-section if it will keep the baby safe. I trust your judgment and know that you have our best interest at heart. I am scared, but we just have to do it scared. In the hands of faith, we fall." Dr. Chung looked at me and nodded. He knows my faith, so he's not shocked at my statement. Someone else would probably be shocked. Oh well. Dr. Chung got up and said that he is going to make arrangements for the surgery. By this time, my mom had been standing there listening to the exchange. She seemed a little worried and walked over to me and sat down holding my hand. "Loreina, do you think this is a good decision? What if something happens during the C-section procedure? Is the baby fully formed at four months?" With all the questions Mom was asking, I was starting to worry like her. So I reassured her, "I think it is a good decision because the baby is in distress because of the severe pains I am having in my lower abdomen. There is always a risk with C-section. It is riskier at this level, but if the baby is in distress while in my womb and has a better chance of living outside of my womb, then C-section is the best alternative. Most of the organs are formed at the four-month stage *(sixteen weeks)*. Now, they are going to schedule the C-section, which will give more time for the baby to keep growing. The baby will be fine. She will be a micro-preemie. She will have to stay in NICU until she reaches her healthy weight to go home and that is about 7.5 pounds." Mom looked reassured now. I breathed a sigh of relief when I saw her muscles relax. I understood her concerns. The same concerns ran through my mind when they mentioned emergency C-section. Dr. Chung had explained it to me, and I remember with Dachon there was a lot of information available from conception to birth.

There is always this place between knowledge and reason. Faith takes residence in between those times. At the end of the day, I just had to rely on my faith in the Lord. I squeezed my mom's hand to reassure her. She gave me a hug.

In that instance, Simi and Dr. Chung came back into the room. Dr. Chung let us know what date was secured for the surgery. "Mrs. Oberon, we have scheduled the surgery.

The good news that it should go smooth because the baby will be at twenty weeks. The bad news is that we were able to secure the date for two weeks from today. We will keep a close eye on you, and the baby making sure we monitor the distress levels. I did schedule a sonogram for tomorrow to check the baby's positioning. As for your hospital stay, we will keep you overnight. Are the severe pains more frequent or far apart? The medicine we gave you should have calmed the pain a bit. About your husband and son, Dr. Friedman informed that he is coming to see you in the next two hours." I listened to him and was nodding yes. I realized that the pain had subsided, and I felt better. In answer to his question, I said, "I am feeling better. The severe pains have diminished. The baby seems calm now. I just hope that we can last for two weeks. It's hard when you are grieving your loved ones and four months pregnant." My mom insisted on staying overnight to watch over me. When I started to think about, it made me wonder if all this will affect my being a good mother. This was going to make things different. I would be different. This loss had changed me. I still ached. I was numb. Wow, it's so scary and so unknown. Dr. Friedman did visit about Nick and Dachon. He informed of the hospital formalities and gave me some documents to sign for the release of Nick and Dachon after preparation. He did let me know that Brandon and Vera were taking care of everything. I thanked him for all he had done for Nick and Dachon. We hugged and he left.

The time came to lay Nick and Dachon peacefully to rest. The funeral mass was celebrated at our parish. The parish was decorated beautifully. We always loved the stained glass windows. They depicted scenes from the Bible. The one behind the altar depicted The Ascension of Christ. Many people attended. Nick touched the hearts of many people, and he touched many lives. The people he helped, his close friends, colleagues, business partners, acquaintances, whole families, and extended families. The mass was beautiful. There was a sense of warm and loving presence throughout the whole ceremony. If we cried, it was because we would miss them but not because they were going to a bad place. We knew in our hearts at that moment that they were with the Lord in heaven. There was sense of knowing that they were with Our Lord in heaven. It seemed as if it was a celebration of eternal life. The funeral mass was just perfection. There were beautiful spring flowers in front of the altar and on the side areas. The choir sang like angels. As the family, we sat in the front pews, first five rows. There was a sense of peace in the background and a sense that we were all consoled by the loving presence around us. The funeral mass ended, and afterwards, we went to the cemetery. There Nick and Dachon were laid to rest in peace and in tranquility.

Later on, everyone was invited to our home for reception. Everyone was so kind offering their condolences. Some brought gifts for the baby, others gifted monies with their cards, and still some helped to clean up. It warmed my heart to see how much Nick had helped a lot of these people. They were so genuine. Brandon and Vera did a superb job. I thanked them and did manage to spend time with them hugging them and consoling them. I told them that they are always welcome to our home regardless. They said they would visit. They asked me how I was doing. And the baby. I told them that I've been fine all day, and the doctor was able to prescribe a safe medication that wouldn't hurt the baby. They knew from prior about the C-section surgery and that I was awaiting the time for it. I wanted the baby to know her father's family because they were wonderful people. I always loved his family and thankful to them for Nick. They were wonderful in-laws. We decided that when the baby was of age, she would go spend summers with them. They agreed.

It was good to see Maxx. He was Nick's twin brother. He was an artist and he traveled around the world creating his masterpieces. Nick often spoke of his brother with a sense of warm love in his voice. When I would ask him about Maxx traveling being a burden to his family, Nick mentioned that he wasn't attached to anyone, so it made it easier for him to travel. Nick would invite Maxx to spend summers with us. I think Maxx loved it. He would say that he had the best of both worlds. I often wondered what he meant by that. Nick wouldn't decode the message. I would think, "Hmmm…twin secrets." One thing I knew is that Maxx loved Dachon so much. When he came to visit us during art show season, he would spend time with them. When Maxx was with Dachon, his face would light up as if he yearned to have his own child. I prayed to the Lord that Maxx would one day have that gift of fatherhood. In the meantime, I always told him that he would be Dachon's wonderful uncle. Maxx looked different now. Sad. Understandably so, he just lost his best friend and his first nephew. His loves. He caught me looking at him. He resembled Nick. Seeing him it's as if Nick was still alive, looking back at me. I looked away with tears welling up in my eyes. I walked over to stand by the window across the room and leaned my head against the side paneling of the window, looking outside. I started crying all over again. Then I felt a strong loving hand on my shoulder. I didn't turn around. I knew it was Maxx coming to console me. He was like that. I could see why he was an artist. His touch was like Nick's touch. So loving and gentle. I couldn't look at him because his features were similar to Nick's accept for his eyes. Maxx's eyes were blue, but they had the same curly dark hair, full lips, high chiseled cheekbones, medium build, and tall in stature; their eyes twinkled when they smiled. I was in my own thoughts, thinking about Nick, when Maxx whispered, "Loreina,

I have some time off. I'll stay with you for a couple of months." I shook my head no, thinking that I'm not going to be a good hostess and would be preoccupied with the baby. He asked in his low tonal voice, "Please, let me. I miss Nick too. I want to be around his things and the people he loved. I want to see the baby and hold her. Please let me stay with you, Loreina. Please." I was thinking, *Oh goodness*. I nodded yes. I said a silent prayer of thanks to the Lord and a prayer for strength. I realized that I'm not the only one grieving for my husband and my son. All these people loved them. I had to be there for them too. When I came to, I turned around and hugged Maxx. I apologized to him for hesitating. "I'm sorry, Maxx, you can stay as long as you want." He looked at me and kissed my cheek and squeezed my hand. We both had a connection with Nick, and that connection was still alive as long as we were. Maxx was always happy when he was with us. This time it would be different. I just prayed for strength. I turned around to look out the window and saw the rosebushes that Nick had planted for me. Nick knew I loved roses, so he planted rosebushes around the house. It's funny because every year for five years he would go to the botanicals show and come home with a new type of rose. He would plant them in the pot first for it to grow its roots and then transplant it to its own flower bed after he prepared it. He had a "green thumb." The roses would bloom like crazy, full of joy, singing in the wind. Now that it's spring, they were in their full bloom. It's odd because it was too early for them to be in full bloom like this.

The day was winding down, and most of the guests had gone. There were a couple of people still there. I told everyone thank-you for coming and that I was retiring for the night. I asked Mom and Marja to set up the guest rooms for Nick's family. They told me everything was done and that I could go and rest. I kissed them thank-you and hugged Nick's family then retired for the evening. Brandon and Vera stayed with us until the baby was born. Harrington the same. He had to return to Chicos Ministry to check on the boys. He wanted to stay longer, but I told him Maxx would be here with me and reassured my brother that he can always call or come visit for a weekend. He agreed to come visit when the baby was born. We hugged and said our good-byes. It was good having my brother here. I'm definitely going to miss him.

The time to have the C-section came, and the surgery was successful. I stayed at the hospital for three days and was released to go home after recovery. We named the baby Evia. We took tons of baby pictures of Evia. I made a resolution to make a scrapbook of Evia's hospital stay. Evia would stay at the hospital for the next five and half months or when she reached seven and half pounds. She was a micropreemie and was put in NICU with three other micropreemies. The hospital room was fairly large; it had a lounge area and two bathrooms. The hospital was very open to families coming to spend time with the tiny babies. They had to be close family members. Each of us would take turns spending time with Evia for the next five months, alternating our schedules. I was on family leave and bereavement leave of absence from my job. To be honest, I don't know if I would return to my job as a technologist. Evia was my top priority, and this focus helped me to cope with life without Nick and Dachon. Now at home and spending time with everyone, we all caught up on old times. Harrington would remind us how Nick made a wonderful impression on the youth at Chico's Ministry. Harrington was a wonderful uncle to Dachon and would send little gifts to him during different sports seasons, his birthday, and Christmas. It was wonderful to remember them. I would retire early each night. Mom and Marja would make sure everyone was well and settled before they retired for the evening.

One morning, I woke up early and ready for the day. The sun's rays were shining through the lace curtains that hung in front of the bedroom window. I noticed how beautiful the sun was. The sunrise gave this early morning glow. So drawn by the sight before me, I walked up to the window and looked down at the rosebushes and felt a warm feeling in my heart. For the first time in a long time, a smile emerged from my lips. Then I thought of Evia. I got ready real quick. I went downstairs; it was still quiet. I think everyone was still sleeping. I wrote a note to Mom and Marja to take care of everyone and that I was at the hospital with Evia. I told them to bring everyone to see Evia.

When I reached the hospital, I went to the NICU. I saw little Evia. She was growing nicely. Pretty soon she would be ready to come home. I have to start preparing her nursery. There's so much to do. My main concern would be to focus on Evia. She was at a delicate time right now.

I was feeding her milk from the bottle now. She drank her milk real nicely. Sometimes she received milk from me as well. I tried to balance it out as best as possible. I prayed to the Lord that I would be a good mom. I really wanted to be a good mom again. Sometimes I'm scared that something would happen. The grieving broke me badly, and I still ache inside from the pains. I just manage them. I still keep in contact with Simi, the bereavement nurse. She had invited me to her bereavement prayer meetings. She said the Lord really helps to heal us in these times. I didn't know she was Christian or the extent of her work. Now it all made sense; she has a strong sense of compassion. I told her I would think about it. She said that a person heals better when they are among people who have gone through the same thing. She said that commonality brings a sense of bond and healing at a higher level. The problem was that I didn't want to go back to that place, and I felt better now. Looking at Evia and taking care of her was healing for me. I didn't think of myself because I had her. I looked at the rosebushes around the house, and I felt Nick's presence in them. I looked at the little drawings and pictures Dachon made at preschool. He was with me. I felt content, and the bouts of pain were few and far between. I was a little scared of them because it still hurts, and sometimes I had to let the hurt feelings pass through then I was strong again. I looked at Evia and told myself that I had to be strong for her because she needed me.

Musing along, I heard a group of people talking outside. Wondering about all the commotion, I opened the door and who do I see? Nick's family coming to visit Evia. I thanked my mom and Marja for bringing them. I hugged them all and greeted them with a kiss on the cheek. They were so warm. I ushered them into Evia and her friends' room. I told them to keep it quiet for the other preemies. I took Nick's parents, Mr. and Mrs. Oberon, over to see Evia. They wore scrubs before approaching Evia's incubator. This was the hospital procedure in order to maintain germ free environment for the preemies. I left them to spend time with their granddaughter. The nurse in charge of the preemies was helping everyone put on their scrubs. Mom and Marja were next to see Evia. Brandon and Vera looked warm and joyful; it was the first time I saw them in this way since hearing the news about Nick and Dachon. I promised to visit them with Evia. I walked over to Mom and Marja while Brandon and Vera cooed over Evia touching her tiny fingers. Evia was so precious. The Lord was answering my prayers through Evia. Dr. Chun said she was healthy and strong. He was at the funeral and offered his condolences. I had an appointment to see him in two weeks. He wanted to take a look at my sutures and stitches. I felt pain every now and then when I was late taking my pain medications. Looking at Mom and Marja, I saw how much Evia was bringing joy into everyone here. Maxx was approaching the incubator. Marja made way for him to approach and touch her through the attached gloves. He was talking sweetly with her, just like he did with Dachon. Evia responded, holding on to the tip of his index finger. It was so sweet to watch. I felt a warm feeling in my heart that I knew he would be a special person in Evia's life. Marja said to me, "He is so wonderful with children. It's a shame he doesn't have one of his own." I nodded. I told Marja that Maxx had asked to stay at the house for a few months. At first I hesitated because with my condition and with Evia, I wouldn't be a good hostess. However, he was grieving his brother's passing and wanted to be around his brother's things and loved ones; it would be consoling to him. I told him he could stay. Besides, it would be good to have people around." Marja nodded with approval. She and Mom liked Maxx too, so I know it wouldn't be a big deal with them.

A New Rose Springs Forward

Every day, Evia grew to be a beautiful little bud. I think her middle name should be Rose. I had to update her papers. Evia had gained four and half pounds and was receiving milk with no problem. Dr. Chance, her pediatrician, said she was doing very well. She was six months now, and her body was still fragile and small; however, she had strong little hands. I couldn't wait to take her home when she's nine months. Her pediatrician said that once she grew to about seven or eight pounds, she would be ready to go home. She still shared her room with three other preemies. They were the same preemies from the very beginning. I had gotten to know their parents, and once and awhile we had lunch together discussing our little precious gems. We also consoled one another when things got tough and when we wanted to take our little ones home and just couldn't. We prayed together, and outside the hospital we texted each other little "pick me up messages." It's really nice to connect with other parents, especially when I'm still mourning the loss of Nick and Dachon.

There were times when my bouts of grief affected me, and they were there to console me back to normal. Thank the Lord for these people. He knew what I needed them at the perfect time. My hope was in the Lord, and my trust was in Him. At this point, I'm walking on water and the Lord was holding His hand out to me. I reached and grabbed His hand every time. The Lord was my main rock, and He brought me little rocks to create a foundation for me. In my mourning, He gave me joy and strength. This, for sure, helped me to remain in His strength.

On the home front, I had two house guests: my mom and Maxx. My mom wanted to stay with me for support because of my mourning and baby Evia. She relieved me with visiting Evia almost every day to give me a break to run errands and took care of other important issues. I was still finalizing my husband's projects, and unfinished business affairs. He had a good few things that he was working on when he passed away. As the surviving spouse, I inherited them. Needless to say, I had taken an indefinite leave of absence from my job as technologist at the local hospital. I couldn't go back to work in the condition that I was in. With Evia in the hospital, as a mom, I would be a wreck worrying about not being able to be near her. It was a burden that the Lord lifted off my shoulders. It felt really good to be in a space of tranquility and grace. This place allowed me to mourn and still have strength to be with Evia. Also, allowed me to take care of my late husband's works and projects he was working on. It seems like yesterday when all this happened. I take it one day at a time.

Maxx had settled in really nicely. He was very comfortable and was taking it easy stabilizing himself. Maxx, being the twin, grieved deeply for his brother. I could see the loss in his eyes. He lost his best friend. Maxx and Nick were inseparable. They grew up together looking after each other through thick and thin. They went to the same boarding schools. They went to the same university. However, they didn't study the same subjects. Maxx was in arts major through and through and received his masters in it. He also minored in music theory. Nick received his MBA specializing in business analysis and minored in organizational leadership. The differences in their personality took them on a separate path where their profession was concerned. Their professions seemed to make up for each other's shortcomings. This was good because it helped their relationship as brothers. It seemed that Nick's profession as a business analyst helped Maxx make good decisions on the business side of his profession as an artist. Maxx, on the other hand, would show Nick the creative side of being a business analyst. It was an angle that Nick did not easily relate to, so it was an asset. They always merged their talents together. I remembered when Maxx first began visiting us; it was during the first year Nick and I were together.

Maxx asked Nick and I to be part of this sketch project he was doing for one of the museums that displayed his work. He explained to us that the museum commissioned him to do this project as part of an overall theme for a show that they were putting on during the winter season. We understood the importance of his work and agreed to be Maxx's subject for this project. The project consisted of a collection of sketch work of Nick and me in different settings. He was able to get a lot of material for this project. The sketch project was called The Two Sets of Being. It was funny because Nick and I had set it up to play a joke on him. So if he was sketching at the park near a lake, Nick and I would pull up the bottom portion of our pants. Maxx would sketch that part. Then we would go in the water and splash water at each other. Maxx would sketch that part. We were like kids, but it was so fun. Another time, Maxx decided to sketch Nick and I having a picnic together. The joke was that we would do everything for real, it wouldn't be staged, but Maxx didn't know this. In his mind we were going to pose through the whole scenery for the sketch work. Well, when we get to the park, we would set up the picnic like normal. Nick and I would start playing around hitting each other with the picnic blanket and chasing each other in the meadow playing "catch me if you can." By this time, Maxx was tired of telling us to stay in position. So he would just give in and start sketching. Finally, we would settle down and set up the picnic area. Spread out the all the food, cutlery, plates, and napkins then motioned for

Maxx to join us. He would tear himself away to join us. Then after we had our picnic and everything was put away, Nick and I would start feeling drowsy so we would lean on each other. Then before you know it, as a joke, he would put his hand on my bare knee and make it seem like we're having "a moment." I 'fell asleep' right away. Mood quickly changed. I woke up from a pretend nap. We would look at Maxx, and saw that he was sketching away like crazy. Then finally, he was done. He said, "You two are something else. If I didn't know better, I think you are trying to sabotage my sketch project." We would look at each other and shake our heads no. (Knowing good and well we were trying to do just that). Finally, we fessed up and told Maxx that we had set up a joke on him. He was like "Oh, really?" So he showed us the sketches, and we were shocked to see that they actually told a story. I guess Maxx wasn't fooled at all. He knew what we were up to. Later on Maxx would let us know that the museum was really impressed with the final sketch work. Maxx sent us photos of it and we were so warm to see how lifelike and impressive sketch project was. We were happy to be part of Maxx's project. We were happy to be his subjects.

Actually, a month later, Nick and I became engaged. The engagement lasted six months which gave us time to prepare for the wedding. Maxx was the best man. Nick always told me that he knew I was the one for him, and he didn't need us to live together to "try it out." So our courtship was a pure one. There was no sexuality. Our romantic moments were really kissing moments. They were sweet. I loved the fact that Nick respected me as a whole woman and didn't have issue with my faith. He embraced it as his own.

He often told me about Maxx. There I learned that Maxx had an outgoing personality that spilled over to his work. His outgoing nature allowed him to interact with people easily, and it showed in his work as an artist. They spoke to each other almost every day. Nick loved Maxx's work and would promote it to all his clients.

Now when I see Maxx grieving, I forget my own grief. He had visited Evia at the hospital. My mom was going away on business for a week, and I was glad that Maxx would be taking over for mom.

One day on a lazy afternoon, I was in the kitchen preparing dinner. I wanted to have a final dinner with all of us before Mom left for her trip. Maxx emerged into the kitchen area from spending time in the studio developing his new art piece. I said, "Maxx, I'm so glad you are taking over for Mom and spending time with Evia. I totally appreciate it."

Maxx, being filled with the warmth of spending time with his niece, says, "Loreina, it gives me great pleasure to spend time with Evia. It's like having my own little daughter. I see Nick in her. She is growing, yet she is also tiny. I like it when she holds the tip of index finger really tight. It warms my heart that she feels secure with me. Loreina, she is a treasure." I looked at Maxx a little surprised at his openness. Like his vulnerable side was finally showing. Maxx has not said much since he had been here. He had retreated into his cell. Everyone mourns differently, and it's understandable. Now it seems as if he is emerging outside of it. It is refreshing to see him open up. I said, "Maxx, I'm so glad you feel that way, and I'm glad that you are sharing. Evia has that special effect on people where you forget yourself when you are with her. It's almost healing in a way. I love her so much. She's my little angel. I'm glad you're taking over for Mom. I'm still working on some of Nick's projects. I was able to complete one them. Now I have three more. One of Nick's projects is to renovate run-down building and turn it into a home for single moms. The building is almost complete, but there's this one permit that we are waiting for. The permit is to install fire sprinklers. Maxx, I would definitely like your input on some of these projects. I also want to talk to you about either donating some of your pieces or creating some from your beautiful imagination in theme of what the building signifies. What do you think?" Maxx, a little taken aback from what I was saying, was silent. He thought, *I didn't realize Nick was so involved in the community. That's what I loved about my brother. I'm going to miss him.* Tears rolled down his face as he stood there.

Loreina, seeing this, closed the distance between them and embraced Maxx. He started to weep. Loreina knew too well the power of grief, but at the same time, she had learned that when others share in it, there's a sense of strength that emerges in the midst.

Maxx whispered, "I'm sorry to shake up like that. Remembering Nick and how compassionate he was just reminds me of how much I miss him. Loreina, I will help you with whatever you need. I'm always here for you no matter what. You are Nick's heart and that makes you my heart too." Maxx rested his cheek on the side of my neck and I felt the tears rolling down his face. I just held him and ran my hand down his back along his spine. This gesture calmed him. I was glad he was calmed. I remember how our grieving seemed to never end. It's only been about four months since we lost Nick and Dachon. I'm so happy Maxx was with us. He was like a part of Nick that gave me strength and support. There was a part of me that was afraid to lean on Maxx too much even though he encourages it. Maxx started to wipe the tears from his cheek and motioned over to sit on the stool at the counter. He said as he settled in, "Loreina, I'm sorry for tearing up again. It's still a little raw." I looked at him completely, understanding where he was coming from. "I understand, Maxx, just know that you are not alone in this. We are getting through together." He nodded yes. Then he said, "So what is the schedule with Evia? What is there to do when I'm there?" Sweet Evia, my other encouragement. I motioned over to the stove and started making preparation to sauté the vegetable in olive oil with some finely chopped garlic. The chicken was roasting in the oven; Cesar salad was in the refrigerator. As

I'm finishing up dinner, I began to update, Maxx, on Evia's progress. Some of it he knew, but the new updates he didn't know yet. "Well, Maxx, Dr. Chung says that Evia grows one-fourth a pound every other day and that pretty soon when she reaches eight pounds, she will be ready to come home. He said that Evia is growing healthy, and there are no complications. You don't know how happy I am to hear that. Evia is seven and half months now. In a month and half, she will be coming home. The next order of business is to get her room ready. So right now, her schedule is visitation 8:00 a.m. to 8:00 p.m. Mom goes to stay with her around 9:00 a.m. and stays with her until 3:00 p.m. or 4:00 p.m. There are times when the nurse will let you feed her. Since you are new to the schedule, she will teach you how. The hospital, for safety's sake, keeps a schedule of who stays with the preemies. Therefore, you would have to sign in when you come to stay with her and sign out when you leave. There is no set schedule, but they like having someone from the family come spend time with her even for a few hours. They say the loving energy helps her stay healthy and grow. Mom stays with Evia on Monday, Wednesday, Friday, and I stay with her the rest of the other days—Tuesday, Thursday, Saturday, and Sunday. You will see the other preemies and their families too. Hey, I was thinking you can bring your sketchbook to make sketches. So what do you think, Maxx? Can you handle it?" I said this with a grin on my face, of course.

Maxx said with twinkle in his eye, "I think it's doable. I like the safety measure that the hospital implements with a sense of order and protocol. It's important to keep the little ones safe. Well, looking forward to learning how to feed little Evia." I have confidence in Maxx; I think he can do it too. This is a stretch for him, and I know that he is doing it for Nick. I have learned to never underestimate people, especially close, loving family.

"Maxx, I have to make sure that Evia's room is ready for her homecoming. That is something that I have to work on tomorrow. Can you stay with her until 4:00 p.m.? During that time, I'll go to the baby store to purchase some things and choose a color for her room. I'm thinking of a combination of pastel pink, yellow, and tan colors for her room. What do you think? I'm going to ask everyone at dinner tonight, so hold that thought."

Maxx nodded, saying, "Well, I myself like warm colors." I finished sautéing the vegetables and set them to stay warm on the stove. The rice pilaf is ready and set to warm. Now it's setting the dining room table. I removed the old tablecloth and placed it with the dirty laundry. I said in response to Maxx, "Yes, warm colors are nice, and they do keep you on the up side of life." I was at the hall closet picking the new tablecloth for the dining room table.

Maxx said, "Well, my dear, I am going to get ready for dinner. See you soon."

I said, "Okay, 'til dinner then." I found a tablecloth that had the colors and decorative designs matching the season we are in. By this time, Maxx had left to prepare himself for family dinner. The tablecloth came with a runner that had tassels, one on each end. The process began with napkins, utensils, crystal glasses, and centerpieces. "Finito." I took a step back and saw the glasses twinkling with the lights coming from the crystal chandelier and a warm feeling crept up. I thought, *Okay, now I need to get ready for dinner. Let me see…Marja, Mom, Maxx, Clara—one of my friends from the preemie club—and Simi are going to be here in the next hour and a half.*

I was ready in an hour and was placing the meals on the table while everyone was in the other room chatting up and getting together. Breathing a sigh of relief, I said, "Finished, thank goodness." I went over to the other room and told everyone, "Okay, it's dinnertime." Everyone came in, took their seats, and sat down at the dinner table. Everyone looked beautiful. When everyone was settled down, we held each other's hand and said grace before eating dinner. There was a sense of quiet, calm, and joy in the room. Everyone's energy was warm. It was a really nice dinner. My mom had tears in her eyes knowing that this dinner was in her honor and I said thanks to her for being here during this rough time. Mom would be back in about two to three weeks, and we were going to miss her until then.

A New Journey For a Little Rose

At the end of the evening, everyone had retired to the other room and were now ready for coffee and cakes. Clara and Simi had left. It was me, Marja, Mom, and Maxx. We sat around telling each other jokes and playing card games. We had finished our last game of cards; and my mom, being the winner, was the star of the evening. Maxx seemed lighthearted and relaxed. Noticing this, I told the others that Maxx was working on some pieces for the upcoming art show. I asked Maxx, "Can you show them the pieces you have finished?" He said, "Sure, Loriena". He got up and brought some of them to show us. Some were of places, others were landscapes, and still some were silhouettes. They each held a meaning and told a story. One piece caught my eye. It was a painting of a young mother and her daughter crossing the river together. I asked Maxx, "Where did you paint this?"

Maxx began to tell us the story of this one, "I had taken a break and had gone to Sweden for a much needed vacation. I was staying in a cottage in the countryside. One day there, I went for a walk in the nearby countryside with my sketchbook in hand. You never know when life moments happen." *(Maxx says that as an artist you want to capture life moments. If you don't, they are gone forever, and you don't get them back. And as an artist, he feels that his life's work is based on these moments and therefore goes on search for them. It gave his work depth and purpose.).* "On my little adventure, I happened to come up to this beautiful blue and clear river. I ran up to it, splashed water on my face, and took a drink. The water was sweet and pure. I drank my fill. When I looked up, I saw this young woman crossing the river holding a child in her arms. Of course, I met her halfway and helped her finish crossing the river. She told me her name was Lillie and her daughter's name was Daisy. They were going home to meet up with her husband. She invited me to dinner with her family as a 'thank-you' for helping cross the river. I told her that I was staying at the cottage about a mile away. She said they always wondered who lived there. I told her that I bought it through a friend and was now using it as a vacation home. We both walked back to the countryside and parted ways to go home with confirmation that I would dine with them the next night at 7:00 p.m. I reassured her that I would. When I reached home, I couldn't get the image of Lillie crossing the river with Daisy in her arms, out of my mind and I started sketching the scene. My mind and thoughts kept going back to the vivid details of that scene. Therefore, I started to paint it oil on canvas.

I painted it with the vividness that my mind would allow me." We were all taken by the story behind the painting. It gave the painting even more depth and character. Especially when you know that these are paintings of real people in real circumstances. Not to say that if they were not real people, but the artist's imagination, that they would be less effective. Art depicts all things and circumstances. That is what makes it interesting and captivating.

Marja said, "Wow, Maxx, I didn't know that your paintings had such depth and reality into them. I always thought that artists painted only from their own imaginations. Never from the realities of life. Are all your paintings drawn from life moments?"

He said, "Not always. There are times when I paint my dreams. Remember, life moments can be your dreams, imagination, other peoples realities. They are called life moments because it is a moment of life that is being played in front of you or happening to you now. Once the moment passes, it cannot be captured again. It becomes history. Your mind, being very intelligent, captures that moment in your memory. Therefore, you are able to replay it in your memory. If we didn't have memory, we would not move forward or learn anything. Your memory is a gift. It teaches you many things. There are times when I paint from memories, which is going to be my next collection project."

I was pretty intrigued by what Maxx was telling us. I said, "Maxx, you are definitely right. Without our memory, we are losing something. There's something good in remembering the past. It is just not staying in the past or dwelling there. You captured it and made something good of it." Maxx looked at me and the others nodding yes. My mom was listening and said that she knew someone in her ministry who was losing their memory and had to rely on pictures to remember her family and friends. It's like without it the person would feel an emptiness, and the familiarity she had with her loved ones would diminish. We all agreed with my mom. We thanked Maxx for sharing his pieces with us and teaching us something. By this time, we all rose and hugged each other with a kiss on the cheek.

I went back into the kitchen and started putting the dishes in the dishwasher. Marja came up after me and started helping me with the dishes. We started talking and catching up on old times. Then, Marja asked me, "How are you doing with Nick not being here? How are you coping?"

I haven't really thought about coping without Nick. The thought of being without him before he passed would have been unthinkable. Now it's a daily life. My eyes started to water at the thought of him not being here with me. I said with a shaky voice fighting back tears, "I, uh, do miss Nick. I wish he was with me. I still have to go through all his belongings, and it is hard. I do it because we have to move forward, and there is Evia to take care of. I have to be strong for her. So I don't dwell too much on it." Marja came over and started hugging me. I began to sob. "Why did it have to happen? Why did he have to take the highway? Why? I miss him and Dachon. It so hard, you know. I just wished that it never happened. It was hard enough having the children, what with all the miscarriages. Nick and I kept thinking that we would only have one child. He would be so happy at seeing Evia. Now he is gone and will never know his beautiful little daughter that he longed to have. He always wanted a boy and a girl. Oh gosh, Marja, it saddens me dearly." Wiping the tears from eyes, I walk to the counter and place the towels on top of the counter. I didn't want to finish cleaning up after dinner anymore. I just wanted to go to bed and rest. I said to Marja, "I can't finish cleaning up. I'm going upstairs to rest."

Marja said, "I can finish cleaning up. You go and rest. You have been on your feet all day preparing this wonderful dinner." I looked over at Marja, thinking what wonderful sister that she is. I am so grateful to have her. She cares so much. I walked over and reached out to hug her.

"Marja, I'm so grateful to have you. I don't know what I would do without the three of you here with me. Between you, Mom, and Maxx, it makes it so much easier to cope." Marja nodded, kissing my cheek. I left the kitchen and went up the stairs to my bedroom. On the way, I bumped into Maxx.

Maxx coming out of his bedroom after putting his paintings away; he heard footsteps down the hallway. The footsteps were getting closer. Maxx walked toward the sound of the footsteps and came upon Loreina coming up from stairway. Seeing her face, I immediately knew' that she was crying again. I am worried about her. I hear her crying almost every night. She basically cries herself to sleep. Each time I wanted to go to her to comfort her, but I stilled myself feeling that it would be an intrusion on her privacy. This time it was different. Seeing her face now gives me great concern for her.

Loreina tried to look away, but Maxx closed the threshold between them and hugged her close. Maxx began to walk Loreina to her bedroom, saying, "Let's get you settled." He took her to the chaise to sit her down and removed her shoes. Then he ran the bathwater, adding some bubble bath soap and bath salt to the water. Maxx knelt down to Loreina and said, "Loreina, you need to relax, and I have made a bubble bath for you. Do you want me to help with anything?" Loreina thought about how thoughtful it is for Maxx to make a bubble bath for her. It's like he knew this was just what she needed.

I said, "No, you did superb already." Maxx, taking the seat on the other side of the room, said, "I'll sit out here while you have your bubble bath." I nodded, went into the bathroom, and closed the door behind me. I undressed and slipped into the warm and soothing bubble bath. Then immediately swooned and let out a sigh. *Wow, I haven't had one of these since New Year's Eve. This is so nice. I can just relax and close my eyes.*

I dried myself with the towel and readied myself for bed. Usually these days its pajamas. Then put on my cotton robe with the moon applique sewn on the left side of the collar. After the bubble bath, I went into the bedroom only to find Maxx asleep on the chaise waiting for me. I stared at him while tears ran down my face again. I remembered how Nick used to love the chaise and would fall asleep on it reading. Seeing Maxx sleeping on it right now, it's like seeing Nick all over again. Memories flooded my mind, and I sat on the bed and lay there weeping. Then I felt a hand my shoulder, and I stopped weeping. I turned around and saw Maxx. He was sitting next to me on the bed and looking a little worried.

"Loreina, I heard you weeping, and it woke me. I couldn't help but comfort you. This is a painful time for all of us. I know it tears you apart to be without Nick. I know my being Nick's twin brother doesn't help it any better. Maybe, I should go. It might be easier for you if I left the house and stayed at my house in Miami. I can still come up and stay with Evia like we discussed."

I was surprised to hear him say this. I definitely don't want Maxx to leave. "Maxx, I don't want you to leave. It helps me tremendously with you being here. I think it helps that you are here. I know you said that you wanted to be near Nick's things to help your grieving. I think we need you, and you need us."

Maxx sat next to me, and I put my head on his shoulders. Maxx whispered in my ear, "Okay, Loreina, I won't leave. You're right we all need one another. I just felt like maybe I was being selfish by being here with you. I felt that maybe you wanted to grieve alone. My resembling Nick doesn't help either." I looked at Maxx and know he was partially right, but there's a greater part of me that wanted us to weather this storm together. It is good that he resembled Nick because it reminded me that part of Nick is with us. I felt like we are a family, and we should be with one another, consoling each other. Tired from the whole day, I started feeling drowsy; and by this time, Maxx was hugging me close to himself. I fell asleep leaning on his shoulder.

Maxx looked down and saw Loreina asleep; he picked her up, threw the covers aside, and placed her on the bed. He positioned her comfortably and replaced the covers over her. He bended down and kissed her forehead. Maxx walked across the room to the door and turned around with one last glance and wondered, *Nick sure knew how to pick them. Loreina is not only beautiful on the outside. She was a beauty within. Such a kind-hearted woman and loving mother. Nick would be so proud of her. My own heart moves for her. No woman has ever moved my heart.* Maxx closed the door to Loreina's room behind him and went to his own room. Once inside, he changed to his pajamas and slipped under the covers himself. Maxx, not much of a praying man, said a little prayer to the Lord, "Lord, thank you and help me on my first day with my little niece, Evia, tomorrow." Then he drifted off to sleep.

Morning came, awakening nature with its sunlight and sweet sounds. Nothing like the fragrance of the morning life to wake up the senses. I felt a warmth on my face and opened my eyes. I quickly squinted my eyes to the rays of the sun coming through the lace draperies from the window above the sleigh bed I was laying on. I rolled over to the side, wanting to sleep the morning away. *Since Maxx was going to start the new schedule with Evia today, and Marja was taking Mom to the airport, I had the morning off to sleep a little.* Then, I heard a knock at the door. "Come in, I'm awake." It was Marja and Mom. Mom came to say good-bye. I got out of bed as they walked into the bedroom. I walked over to Mom and gave her a big hug. "Thank you so much, for being here, Mom. I know you are only going to be gone two to three weeks, but we are going to miss you a lot." We hugged and kissed each other on the cheek. I hugged Marja, and they left. I slipped back onto my bed under the covers and took a morning nap.

I woke up late morning and started getting ready for the day. I walked down the stairs to the kitchen; I felt relaxed and energized a little. Today was going to be Evia's day because I had to get her room prepared for her homecoming. I definitely needed a baby interior designer to help with new ideas and find a nice theme for Evia's room. The room was going to be next to mine. Her room would be warm and allow her to be free. It would be her little sanctuary. Everything would be organized to make it easy for everyone to find Evia's things. Colors of the room would be pastel with a fresh look. Definitely add beautiful window treatments to accentuate the colors of the room. Evia's baby furniture would be made of light-colored wood. Her first bed would be a bassinette, then a crib, two dressers, changing table with wheels, and storage units for her miscellaneous baby things. Her closet of course would hold all her clothes and shoes. Since baby clothes and shoes are small, the closet would more likely be her storage space for now. It would also keep her stroller, baby walker, and baby toys. The flooring would be plush carpeting and would place a plastic mat under the rolling changing table area. Or could make the area tiled and put carpeting around it. The changing table would come with baby tub; therefore, the mat (or tile) would keep the water from splashing over to the carpet. Since I have these ideas listed on paper, all I need now is the baby interior designer to help me put it all together. I am going to put a bassinette in my room for Evia. She would stay in the bassinette for couple of months or until she outgrows it. Then transport her to the crib.

Looking through the phone book, I booked an appointment for tomorrow with three interiors designers that specialized in designing nurseries: one at 10:00 a.m., second at 1:00 p.m., and third at 3:00 p.m. I told each exactly what I was looking for, and they were putting together a presentation for our meeting. This was how I managed things. It made things run smooth and streamlined. I knew that there were things that were beyond my control, and whatever I can work with, I do. I thanked the Lord every day that I have wonderful and loving people in my life right now. It would not have been easy without them. If Maxx didn't step up and really cooperated to help me with Evia today, taking care of fixing her room for her homecoming would be very difficult. I knew that I'm leaning on him a little heavy now but had to go with it and be thankful for the blessing. I knew beyond a shadow of a doubt that somehow in the greater scheme of things the Lord had His beautiful hands all over it, and it warmed my heart so much to know this. I hope Maxx was doing okay on his first day with Evia. I picked up my cell phone to call Maxx. It rang a few times, and no one picked up. Oh, I remember. Cell phones were not allowed in the hospital. Thank goodness, I had Evia's phone number for her room. I called that and someone answered. It may be the preemie nurse.

"Hi, this is Loreina, Evia's mother. Is there a gentleman named Maxx there?"

She said, "Hi, Loreina, this is Ruth. Yes, Maxx, the handsome man is here. He takes direction well. We have been teaching him the ropes, and Evia is really taking it well. I will get him for you."

I said, "Thank you."

Maxx came to the phone. "Hi, Loreina, how's it going? Did you rest well? You looked exhausted last night and was a little concerned. I figure you needed my brother-in-law expertise."

Laughing, I said, "I'm doing very well. Yes, I rested well. Marja took Mom to the airport. I took a morning nap then spent the day making plans to get Evia's nursery ready for her homecoming. I have to call her doctor to find out the exact date. How is she doing, Maxx? How are you doing?"

Maxx answered, "It's been an interesting day. The nurses have been teaching me and helping with Evia. I also met a parent of one the other preemies. This place is really friendly, and I like the security. Evia is doing very well. She has grown a lot from the last time I saw her. I think the nurse said that she is 7.5 lbs and 5 ounces. She has been eating well. When she wakes up, I talk to her, and she holds my index finger with her whole little hand while I'm talking to her. She is making little baby noises. It really warmed my heart to be with her today. Me, I'm really doing well. I slept good last night. It was the first time in weeks since Nick and Dachon passing. Being here with Evia is really refreshing. She is something special. She makes me feel strong and more alive. It's as if being here with Evia is therapeutic. Like a sense of calm."

Listening to Maxx say that confirmed to me that this child was special. I felt the same thing that Maxx was feeling. "Maxx, I feel the same way when I am with her. My mom and Marja have said the same thing too. Being around Evia is therapeutic. If you weren't feeling well, you will feel well. If you are grieving, you receive a sense of strength and consolation. If you were not in a good mood walking in, your mood changes to joy and happy after you enter the room. There is definitely something special about her. Maybe because she is a miracle. Maxx, I hope to be a really good mom to her."

Maxx, sensing the worry in Loreina's voice, said, "You know, you were a wonderful mom to Dachon and a wonderful wife to Nick. I always saw how loving and caring you were with them. You are pretty amazing woman, and Nick would be proud of you. You have nothing to worry about. Besides, you have me, Marja, and your mom." Maxx was right, I shouldn't worry. Things would work out. "Thank you, Maxx. I couldn't have had a better brother-in-law. Well, I'm going to let you go. I'll see you later. Give Evia a kiss for me. See you soon! Bye, Maxx."

Maxx, feeling better that Loreina was calm, said, "Okay, I'll see you later, and I will give Evia a kiss for you. Bye, Loreina."

We both hung up together. I decided to go to daily mass today. I needed to be close to the Lord and just be present to Him. I haven't been to daily mass since Nick and Dachon funeral service. I had been preoccupied with Evia. She was born so small, and my main focus had been her. I had been praying during the day and getting into my daily devotionals. Sacred Scripture always lifted me up and kept me going. When I reconciled with the Lord five years ago, the Lord inspired a closer relationship with Him. This inspiration helped me to learn about my faith and learned more about Christ. The Lord showed me the road to having a close relationship with Him. He helped me get my priorities in order by putting Him first. I remember asking the Lord to be patient with me because I had been through a lot in my life and needed His love and patience. The Lord, being the gentleman that He is, definitely obliged. Therefore, my allegiance with the Lord was a definitely wonderful and good. It was one of the best decisions that I ever made in my life. This decision had been nothing but blessings through and through.

A Hiccup On the Road to Life

Service was wonderful as usual. Receiving the Lord in communion and spending quality time with Him was also amazing. I felt renewed and refreshed. There were still some deep healing that I had to allow the Lord to work in me, but now, this was good for me. After service, some people were asking me how I'm doing and offering their condolences. I was really touched by them. I forgot that sometimes my parish community can be a source of support. Couple of people did call me to offer their condolences and if I needed anything to let them know. I just hadn't been needing anything lately. I did have a couple of friends at the parish that I can invite to Evia's homecoming get-together. I was part of two ministries and have had to call their leader to let them know that I am taking a break to grieve. They understood what was going on, and they were very supportive and told me to take my time. It was refreshing to hear. I knew it was an authentic gesture. Sometimes people can be unauthentic, and I don't have the time or the energy to deal with them.

Evia's nursery is almost done. The interior designer who specializes in nurseries that I hired was doing a great job. She took my ideas and made something wonderful out of them. She also added her own touches, which I thought went well with my ideas. Evia is going to have a whimsical sweet nursery to go with her little beautiful self. Looking around the room, seeing the beautiful mural of the animals with little captions above their heads conversing with one another on the walls, is a sight to see. There was a mural of cloud-filled sky on the ceiling, and it's funny because if you look really close up there were little angels sitting on the clouds. Some had harps in their hands, some were sleeping, and others were just being playful. It was really a sweet image. The colors in their wonderful pastels (pink, yellow, and blue) perfectly compliment the decor. The nursery furniture were superbly positioned in a way that would make it easier to move around the room without bumping into anything. The walls were sporadically decorated with baby decor *(blocks, teddy bears, and alphabet letters)*. The whole decor was sporadic not everything was bunched up together, and I really liked that. She also placed a rocking chair next to the crib. It's a must that I forgot to add into my plans. She also suggested that I have another rocking chair in my room next to the bassinet since Evia will be staying there for the next couple months. Of course, I agreed.

Now it was time to plan Evia's homecoming get-together. It's going to be on a Saturday, and I wanted to invite all the people that were involved in taking care of her. This was really stretching me because through all this, I was thinking about how much Nick would have been part of all this, preparing her nursery and planning her first party. Dachon would be underfoot tagging along being my four-year-old little helper, seeing their smiling faces. It is hard to not just crumble and just not do the homecoming get-together. If I did that, people would understand, which is so wonderful for them to be supportive. However, when I think about how tiny Evia was when she was born and that she was born so early, five months to be exact, it just seemed like I wanted to thank them for being there with me through this journey to make sure Evia grew healthily. Her making it this far and coming home was short of a miracle. I prayed a lot to keep Evia and to give me strength through this. This was such a raw and vulnerable moment right now, but the Lord was ever so faithful in sustaining me.

I wanted to hire a caterer to prepare the meal for the homecoming get-together. They would come and set up and prepare the whole meal. Then they would also clean up after everything ended. I wanted everyone to just relax and wind down, not feeling like they have to do anything.

Evia's homecoming was approaching. It was going to be around Thanksgiving time. The homecoming get-together was next on the list to plan. I planned to invite everyone that had been part of Evia's life as she has entered into the world as a micro-preemie. The people would include the preemie club and nurses assigned to her and the other preemies at the hospital. The homecoming dinner was gesture of thanks to honor all the people who took care of Evia and the preemies. There will be other people there that I want to invite who have been supportive through my grieving Nick. Nick's whole family would be there of course. I miss Brandon and Vera. We do keep in touch every week. Vera, in a matter of fact, was planning to stay for a month during Christmas time. All in all, it should be about twenty-five to thirty people. Let say thirty people for now. The planning will consist of decor, dinner meals, invitations, and catering company to setup and serve the guests. I took out my pad and starting jotting down all the details when I heard the phone ring around 4:00 p.m. I rushed to pick up the phone; it was Maxx on the other end. A thought ran through my mind, *He should be getting off from watching Evia around now. I hope all is well.*

Maxx, on the other end, said, "Loreina, are you busy right now? There had been some complications with Evia and another preemie, Jamie. Dr. Chung had been here for the last half hour with them. It looked like Evia had a problem with a new formula that they started giving her today. The nurse informed me that it is normal procedure and that newborns and preemies usually respond well to the new formula. I didn't think nothing of it and gave the okay. The nurse said that since Evia had not had any colic symptoms that it would be okay. The reason I didn't call right away was because Dr. Chung wanted me to stay nearby explaining what was happening. Dr. Chung was stabilizing Evia and Dr. Waverly was stabilizing Jamie." I was pretty shocked to hear and just felt worried that Evia stays strong. She had come so far without any problem. Thank goodness Maxx was there. Imagine if no one was there to watch over Evia. I hope Jamie was doing well. I know his mother worked late a lot and sometimes there was no one to watch over him.

Addressing Maxx, I said, "Maxx, I will be there as soon as I can. Thank you for calling me." I quickly said good-bye to Maxx and placed the phone on its receiver. I fetched my coat, keys, purse, and got into the car to drive to the hospital. On my way there, I called Mom and Marja to let them know what happened. They were both concerned.

I reached the hospital and showed my badge to the security guard while heading to the elevator. The hospital gives patients' families security badges since their visit may include overnight sleep or daily visits while the patient or preemie recovers. It's all part of the sign-in process that they have. I took the elevator to the twelfth floor preemie unit. The elevator ride seems like forever. Finally, I reached the twelfth floor. Maxx was there waiting, and I saw Jamie's mom speaking with Dr. Waverly. I walked over to Maxx, and we walked over to Dr. Chung. He started to explain why Evia had a negative reaction. Dr. Chung said, "I'm glad you're here, Loreina. We normally switch the formula for newborns and preemies when they reach seven pounds.

Since Evia and the other preemies have taken the formulas pretty well, we thought it would be safe to switch them. After ten minutes of being on the new formula, Evia and Jamie started to turn red and regurgitating the formula. Maxx noticed what was happening and notified the nurse right away. We increased fluid intravenously to flush their systems. They are both stabilized now. We are going to keep a close eye on both of them to make sure the new formula has cleared their system. We are going to put them back on the previous formula, eventually we have to change it."

I listened intently, taking in what he was saying. Maxx and Jamie's mom Karen were listening as well. I'm worried because Evia cannot stay on the same formula forever. Eventually, she had to be weaned off this formula. I guess Dr. Chung must have read my thoughts. He began to explain, "Right now, we are trying to find another formula to move them into while they are still on the previous formula. We should have another one available by the end of the week."

I asked Dr. Chung, "Why are you changing their formula?" I had an idea but was not sure and thought to ask him. Dr. Chung answered, "Since they are growing and developing, the formula they are on does not have some of the nutrients that their bodies need. The new formulas have these nutrients and we start them on it when they reach seven pounds. This does not happen all the time, but when it does we try to care of it right away." I felt reassured. It seemed like the hospital had it all under control. I know that there are times when you cannot control everything. I'm just glad that the Lord is watching over Evia. Maxx seemed relaxed and Karen the same. Dr. Waverly returned to our room where we were standing. "Hi, everyone and Dr. Chung, we are checking on the other new formula. I'm sure Dr. Chung has explained to you what has happened. It is nothing to worry about because on the low occasions that it happens we have another alternative formula that we are going to try. Before we try it, we are running tests to find out what made them have that reaction and make sure the new formula does not have that substance. There are two formulas that we move them to. This is a precaution in cases like today."

Karen didn't seem reassured. "What if this happens with all the new formulas? What do we do then?"

Both Dr. Chung and Dr. Waverly looked at her a little surprised. We were waiting for their answer. Dr. Waverly said, "We have not had that problem, but if it happens, we will keep them on the formula that maintains their health. There are foods that have nutrients that the preemies need to continue growing and developing that we can put them on. These same foods will be on a list given to their parents when they are ready to go home. We are going to keep an eye on them and make sure that they are returned to good health before we discharge them to go home. Does anyone have any more questions?" We all looked at each other and shook our heads no. Dr. Waverly said that he had to check on some of his other patients and wished us safe journey home. He left. Jamie's mother said thank you to Dr. Chung and went to say good-bye to Jaime. Maxx and I said thank you to Dr. Chung. We told him that we appreciate both him and Dr. Waverly for all their efforts in stabilizing Evia and Jamie. He said it's their job, and they want to make sure that the babies are in good health. Maxx and I thanked him. He said that he would return the next day to check on Evia. We both nodded okay. Dr. Chung left. Maxx and I went over to Evia to spend time with her. I put on the robe and special gloves. Evia was in a bigger incubator now. She looked stable and normal. I'm so glad that she is okay. I said a thank-you to the Lord for watching over her and the preemies. Life is so fragile. At any given time something can happen. I'm so glad that Maxx was here to watch her while I was home making preparations for Evia's homecoming. I could not help but think of history repeating itself. I just knew beyond a shadow of a doubt that the Lord would not give me more than I can handle. Since Evia was sleeping and it was getting to be early evening, I wanted to leave her be. There were two nurses in NICU to watch over them, and it gave me reassurance at leaving Evia. The nurses here were great and compassionate people. I let Maxx know. He was agreeable and wanted to let Evia sleep through the evening. Tomorrow was my turn to spend the day with Evia. It is great because I can work on the blanket that I was knitting for her and spend some time in prayer with the Lord in the chapel. It is good!

Sweet, Sweet Homecoming

Evia was doing well and adjusting to the new formula. Dr. Chung had found formula that was sensitive to babies' digestive system, and Evia was adjusting to it very well. Jamie was the same. He was responding to the new formula very well. All the invitations had gone out to everyone on the list. The RSVPs were coming in. Brandon and Vera, Evia's grandparents were flying in for the week. They were so excited about Evia. During the whole time I kept in touch with them keeping them up to date about her. Vera had sent me a lot of baby items: clothes, shoes, bedding, bottle set complete with caddy, bath supplies. It was really nice. I had decided that the homecoming would be a baby shower as well. It made sense, and it was easier to plan this way.

There are times when you have to celebrate life and in doing that you start to build something wonderful that attracts the ones around you. It can be contagious. Evia's journey had been a long one. Born so delicate and fragile at a moment that was filled with grief and loss. She was the spark of light that was here with us. She was the light that kept us grounded so that grief and loss did not take us into a space that would keep us stagnant and never gaining hope to carry us through. Evia's diminutive form brought a greater perspective into each person that touched her and that she touched. The sacrifices that each person made to spend time with her did not go unnoticed in the greater scheme of things. A sense of change was moving us forward. Losing Nick and Dachon was pretty devastating. What made it devastating was that Nick and Dachon would never meet her. So every day that I spent time with Evia help me to not think of it that way. I chose to think that Nick and Dachon was watching over Evia in heaven. I felt that they were helping her push through these months and giving all of us the strength to do it. It is as if the Lord was helping us from heaven and helping us from earth. Nothing is a mistake because there is something wonderful that is greater than us that does make itself present when we are at those turning points in life. Losing my precious Nick and Dachon was a major turning point in my life. I didn't know how to turn the corner. When I went to the Lord to pour into Him to help me through this, I didn't know what to expect. What happened was pretty amazing, and with Evia, I was able to turn the corner with a little joy that continues on. When I turned the corner, there were people on the other side standing there with their arms open waiting to help us get through this. This is what happens when we give ourselves with all our stuff over to faith. Faith takes them and turns them around to something wonderful.

The homecoming was in three days, and I was going to the hospital to sign Evia's release papers. Evia was almost eight pounds. She had come into her own where you can see her face take form. She had beautiful black curly hair, hazel eyes, and full lips. She was twelve inches. She had all five fingers and toes. Dr. Chung and Dr. Waverly have both given her a clean bill of health. I brought with me all that I needed to bring Evia home. In the last minute, I had decided to bring her home couple days before the celebration. It was to let her get settled in and allow her to be in a new environment. In hindsight, I wanted her with me as soon as possible. Missed my precious little one and couldn't wait to hold her in my arms bonding with her, being a mommy to her.

All the paperwork was done. The nurse had readied Evia; therefore, she didn't have any tubes attached to her. The nurse placed her in the baby stroller. We wheeled her out with the big baby bag and big teddy bear with balloons. The car was in the hospital driveway, and we were able to transfer the baby to the car seat. The nurse helped me to place the stroller into the car. I came to do this by myself because I insisted for everyone to stay home making the finishing touches on all the decor and preparation for the celebration. We drove home and the hospital was finally behind us. We were looking forward to a new life in a new place called home.

The day of the celebration came. Everything was as it should be. The catering company was here prepping for dinner. They set up the dining area as well as the patio area outside where the guest would gather for non-alcoholic cocktails. The catering company had an in-house bartender that could make the most amazing non-alcoholic drinks. So I decided to set up a small bar where people can order their cocktails based on their favorite fruit. On the invitations, I included the menu with mention that only nonalcoholic cocktails would be served. I did this because this wasn't an adult party; it was a celebration for a new life who survived the most delicate beginning of her coming into the world. Miraculously enough everyone RSVP'd and said couldn't wait to come. Looking around, I saw the whole house was decorated very festively. It was fall season, so the theme was fall-inspired baby themed streamers covering the ceilings from room to room. Baby party favors were sprinkled all over the tables. The first floor of the house was just magnificent. The whole family was here. Everyone made it. Mom, Marja, Harrington, Maxx, Brandon, and Vera. They also helped me put all the finishing touches that were needed in place.

Time was here and the guests were trickling in. Everyone had their post. Vera and I were the hostesses meeting everyone at the entrance. We had two assistants helping us when we noticed guests bearing gifts. Evia was receiving gifts, greeting cards, or gift bags filled, and teddy bears. Mom and Marja were hostesses meeting them at the entrance to the patio to show them out to the large deck area. Harrington and Maxx were in charge of making sure everything went smoothly and assisting the caterers. Brandon was in the music room playing the piano, serenading the guests as they walked by to go to the porch area. Some guests decided to sit inside the music room, just relaxing and allowing themselves to be entertained. Brandon's little concert was just the icing on the cake. Ahhh! The gift of music. *(Thank goodness Harrington and Maxx thought to set up chairs in there earlier, just in case.)* Nick had constructed the music room to play the piano with Dachon. Now I know who taught Nick how to play. Tears were welling up in eyes just thinking about it. Well, wouldn't you know, my brother Harrington caught me at this moment. He came up to me and hugged me, saying, "Loreina, everything is going to be okay. Remember, Dachon and Nick are in heaven watching over us." I nodded yes, but inside I missed them. I was glad our family was here together and that was all that mattered. Evia was dressed so beautifully for her celebration. Pretty soon everyone here would meet this precious gem of ours. Everyone including the preemie club was here. Their preemies were leaving the hospital at different times, and we promised each other to attend each other's homecoming celebrations. The evening was getting underway. Everyone was here now and just enjoying themselves at the patio and the music room. I sent Maxx to gather everyone into the dining area for dinner. Every came and sat down for dinner. Brandon led us in saying grace before dinner. Thanking the Lord for getting us over the most difficult year. It was fall now, but the rest of the year seemed clear ahead. Everyone was enjoying dinner and laughing and just being themselves. It was beautiful sight.

The evening went smoothly. Each of us thanked everyone for coming and being part of Evia's life. I told them the story of Evia and her little journey to remain with us. I thanked all the people that helped her to stay strong either by taking care of her or spending time with her or feeding her and all the aspects of sharing their compassionate nature with her. Some people wanted to share what it meant for them when they spent time with Evia and the preemies. It was touching to hear how Evia and the preemies affected these people. By this time, I had brought Evia downstairs to meet everyone. She was safely tucked in her bassinet. It turned out to be a wonderful celebration. Brandon was able to lead everyone to sing while he played the piano. Maxx also uncovered his new collection titled, *Life at Its Best*. The collection was tribute to his niece, Evia. It shows her in her stages from birth to now. It shows her journey and the one to come. The moment was jovial. It echoes in my heart that the life we have is meant to be shared and given freely so that it continues on before us.

"Come to me, all you who labor and are
burdened, and I will give you rest.
Take my yoke upon you and learn from me,
for I am meek and humble of heart; and you
will find rest for yourselves. For my yoke is easy,
and my burden is light."

Matthew 11:28-30 (NAB)

Lightning Source UK Ltd.
Milton Keynes UK
UKOW07f1452141214

243121UK00012B/130/P